Blue Skies & Gunfire

K. M. PEYTON

DEFINITIONS

BLUE SKIES AND GUNFIRE
A DEFINITIONS BOOK 978 1 862 30157 3

First published in Great Britain by David Fickling Books,
a division of Random House Children's Books
A Random House Group Company

David Fickling Books edition published 2006
Definitions edition published 2008

1 3 5 7 9 10 8 6 4 2

The Random House Group Limited supports the Forest Stewardship Council (FSC), the
leading international forest certification organization. All our titles that are printed on
Greenpeace – approved FSC – certified paper carry the FSC logo. Our paper procurement
policy can be found at: www.rbooks.co.uk/environment

Mixed Sources
Product group from well-managed
forests and other controlled sources
www.fsc.org Cert no. TT-COC-2139
© 1996 Forest Stewardship Council

Set in 12/15pt New Baskerville

Definitions are published by Random House Children's Books,
61–63 Uxbridge Road, London W5 5SA

www.**kids**at**random**house.co.uk
www.**rbooks**.co.uk

Addresses for companies within The Random House Group Limited
can be found at: www.randomhouse.co.uk/offices.htm

THE RANDOM HOUSE GROUP Limited Reg. No. 954009

A CIP catalogue record for this book is available from the British Library.

Printed in the UK by CPI Bookmarque, Croydon, CR0 4TD

To Anne and Irene

Author's Note

I have never written about anything set in the Second World War before, although I lived through it during my most impressionable years, from the age of ten to sixteen. I lived on the outskirts of London and saw much of the Battle of Britain in the sky above. I was on a train going to school which was machine-gunned, and had to shelter under trees a few times out in the country from a Spitfire, flying very low, shooting up a Messerschmitt, or vice versa. I was not evacuated until the time of the doodlebugs, when I went to an aunt in Birmingham after school broke up for the summer holidays. The doodle-bugs were terrifying, but I actually enjoyed the excitement of the rest of it. We were not bombed out, luckily, although we had all our windows blown in, and my school was very knocked about. In winter we had lessons wearing all our outdoor clothes, including gloves, for there were no windows and no heating. We all had terrible chilblains.

So this book, although fictitious, is written with a lot of true things in it. I did have a very romantic, innocent affair with a man ten years older than myself who was wireless operator/gunner in a bomber. He flew on raids over Germany night after night and was shot down once, parachuting into the sea. He was very lucky to stay alive. His brother, a pilot, was killed. He proposed to me under the cherry blossom in Kew Gardens. I have never forgotten him.

Nowadays, in this era of fantasy, books are written blithely about settings the writer has never experienced. We can write today about places we have never been to. I do it myself now I see everyone else doing it, and have just recently 'been' to Australia. I would never have dared to do this fifty years ago. With this in mind it occurred to me that it was an awful waste of material not to write a book set in a very special period with which I am perfectly familiar. So, after all this time, for better or for worse, here it is.

K M Peyton

Chapter One

They lay in the grass on Wimbledon Common, under some birch trees where the bracken grew, where no one could see them. Occasionally horse riders went by on the gravel track beyond the bracken and they saw the legs passing, the hooves pressing into the soft gravel, heard the riders' voices, laughing. The sky was blue, unclouded, some fighter trails crossing very high.

'I love you,' said Sidney.

Josie laughed. 'Only till you join up. And if you love me, why are you so anxious to join up and go away?'

'Oh, you can't miss that sort of thing. I can still love you when I'm a soldier.'

'Lucky you're too young.'

'I'm going to give the wrong age next time. Ernie Pearson got in that way.'

'By next time we'll all be Germans. They're nearly here.'

'Rubbish!'

'I saw my father get an old pitchfork out of the

1

garden shed last night. He's propped it up by the kitchen door.'

'Crikey! A pitchfork! Give me a kiss, before the Germans get you.'

He leaned over her, his shiny black hair falling over his white, eager face. Her mother said he was common. So what? Josie liked the feel of him. He was warm and sweet and smelled of oil. He had an Ariel Red Hunter motorbike.

'Do you love me?' he insisted.

'Not really.' If she encouraged him he started putting his hand up her blouse and she didn't like that. Her mother said she must never let a boy touch her, not inside her clothes. Never, *never*. She mustn't get a baby, whatever happened. They would have to leave the neighbourhood.

To change the subject she said, 'Anyway, I'm going away. I'll be gone before you join up.'

'Going away! Where to? What for?'

'In case the Germans come. To somewhere safe. Safer, anyway. To my Auntie Betty in Essex.'

'Oh, only Essex. That's not very far. I can come up on my bike.'

'North Essex. Deep country. I've been there. It's awful.'

'I'll come. The Germans won't find you. But I will.'

Here came his hand again, rummaging inside her blouse. He was bad at buttons.

'Gerroff! You'll tear it!'

She sat up abruptly.

'I thought you loved me,' he wheedled.

'Not like that. Just kissing and that. You can kiss me. Not go in there.'

They rolled about in the grass, kissing and nibbling and laughing. After a bit she began to wish his hand would come again, but she knew that that was the time to go. Her mother had put the fear of God into her.

'They only want one thing!' her mother snorted.

She never stipulated what that thing was, only that they should never get it.

Josie stood up, shaking the grass off her skirt. She was still in school uniform. Whatever would her head-mistress say? Eating in the street was forbidden; rolling in the grass (in uniform) would be completely beyond the pale. Sidney had met her out of school, round the corner. Their affair, if that is what it could be called, was fairly clandestine, as Josie's mother thought Sidney unsuitable. She thought Josie should choose a nice boy from the local public school, who would raise his cap when he called and say, 'Good evening, Mrs Marsden.' She disliked the oily boy on the motorbike who rode down the street tooting, his greasy hair flapping over his goggles. She did not know he took Josie out on the bypass and went at eighty miles an hour. Josie thought he was a laugh.

They walked back through the trees, holding hands.

It was May and the birches trembled with new leaf in the late afternoon sun. This was the only country Josie knew and at times like this she thought she could like the country. But she was an urban, London girl.

She knew hot pavements and rattling tube trains, the airless museums they trailed round on Sunday afternoons, the picture galleries, Lyons Corner Houses and the ducks in St James's Park. She couldn't imagine it filled with German soldiers. But then the Parisians didn't think of Paris like that either, nor did the Dutch of Amsterdam, the Belgians of Brussels.

'I don't think they'll come,' she said hopefully.

'No. The Channel's in the way. How can they?'

Sidney was a simple soul of little imagination. He saw being a soldier as beer and camaraderie and a bit of excitement. He knew he would enjoy it. Josie knew that if he enlisted, he would forget her. It was quite simple. She didn't care.

'So where've you been, miss?' her mother asked sourly when she walked in.

'I was kept in,' she lied easily. She did not lie about big things, but little things – it saved a lot of trouble.

Her mother wasn't easy to love. Their house was down the hill, not in the posh part near the common, but in a street of tight little Victorian houses where net curtains hid the goings-on and neighbours had to be impressed. Not to give the neighbours anything to talk about was Mrs Marsden's object in life, and having an attractive sixteen-year-old daughter was beginning to prove a strain.

'The sooner you go up to your Auntie Betty's the better,' she said. Josie guessed she had noticed the grass clinging to her skirt.

'You're sending me away because of Sidney – nothing

4

to do with the war!' Josie shrilled. 'It's not fair!'

'Just take a bit of notice of what's going on, for goodness' sake,' her mother replied.

She pushed a newspaper across the table where she was laying tea. The headline read 'EVACUATION OF TROOPS FROM DUNKIRK'. Underneath it said, 'This is the end of the British struggle to keep the Germans at bay.'

'There's nothing to stop them invading now,' her mother said bitterly. 'France never put up a fight! We sent all those troops across to help them and what good did it do? Now the poor devils are being pushed into the sea, trapped like rats. They're sending ships to rescue them – what a farce! A total disaster. There's nothing to stop the invasion now – we're the only country left. And all you can think of is Sidney! For heaven's sake, girl, grow up.'

Josie was taken aback by her mother's vehemence.

It was true that she was totally occupied by her own affairs and mostly ignored the news. Her family, unusually, had no relations or close friends in the forces so there were no anxieties in that department. There were the strange inconveniences: having to dig up half the garden to install an Anderson shelter, being fitted with a gasmask and having to carry it everywhere you went – funny things rather than ominous. Gasmask practice at school was a laugh a minute: crashing snouts, steaming up, making wonderful farting noises by breathing out hard . . . nobody ever gave a thought to the possibility of having to use a gasmask in earnest. Josie loved school, which was just down the road and full of good friends. She was clever and had passed eight subjects in the School Certificate the year before and was now just kicking her heels in the sixth form before she started at art school in the autumn. No pressure. Her school had given up on her since she had shown her determination to study art. 'What a waste, with your brain!' they fumed, only interested in sending out their 'gels' to be missionaries, doctors, nurses or teachers. To serve the community was the object of the education instilled with such zeal. Being an artist meant joining the ne'er-do-wells, the immoral 'Bohemians' who lived nefarious lives mostly in Paris. But Josie had surmounted the antagonism with the same bland indifference with which she was now so annoying her mother. 'All you think of is yourself!' The scorn was a familiar cry. It rolled over her.

But, looking at the photograph on the front of the paper, it occurred to her that her mother might have a point.

'I thought – I thought—' But it was true what her mother said: she hadn't thought at all. Only about what she was doing today, would do tomorrow. The suggestion now that her future might be challenged was a shock.

'Why, what's going to happen? If they come . . .' She couldn't picture it at all. Her father wielding a pitchfork? To stick it in a German soldier? It wasn't in his

6

character, her mild, quiet, law-abiding, office-bound father Joe.

'They'll send the planes in first, to soften us up, and the bombers, to get the upper hand in the air. And then they'll come.'

'But our fighters will stop them!'

'Poor lads, against that might? How can they? There's not enough of them, compared with the Luftwaffe.'

Josie knew her mother was a pessimist by nature, but it hadn't ever occurred to her that Britain wasn't going to win the war. She didn't know what to say. Whining against the decision to send her away suddenly seemed rather petty. She knew her parents were only acting for her safety. Or was it a ploy to dump Sidney?

'It's not very far, Auntie Betty's. Sidney said he can come up on his bike.' Josie challenged her mother, making trouble, which was her habit. Sometimes she knew she was not very nice – quite often, in fact. She didn't know why she did it. But her mother needled her. She was a sour woman, given to running people down. She hadn't many friends. But she was very strong, and not given to showing emotion. They rarely kissed in their family and her mother's idea of a cuddle was a quick bony hug, more like a spur of encouragement than gentle comfort.

'The sooner he's in the army the better. I can't see what you find in him – he's no brain to speak of.'

'Brain's not everything.'

They always argued. It was a habit. Mostly bickering, but sometimes blazing rows.

'It'll do you good to leave home,' her mother said.

'But I must come back when art school starts!'

'That will be in the lap of the gods.'

But when Josie compared notes at school she found that nearly everyone was going away. They said just for the summer holidays – 'until we see what happens'. Quite a lot in her form had already gone. The form below, taking their School Certificates, were mostly hanging in there until the exams were over, then they were nearly all off. It wasn't so bad when you knew you weren't the only one. Most were going down to Devon or Cornwall or up north, so by comparison she wasn't going very far. The school was trying to find premises for a total evacuation into the country, but by that time Josie knew she would have left.

She wasn't the only one who would be parted from her friends. The only one not going anywhere was her best friend Mary. This was because her parents were religious and trusted in God not to get killed, or to get killed, as He willed. Mary was incredibly clever and earmarked for a scholarship to Oxford. In spite of being incredibly clever she adored Biggles books and shared all her Biggles library books with Josie. Biggles was their hero.

'There's a big aerodrome near where you're going,' Mary said. 'You'll see lots of planes.'

They were good at planes, and could recognize them all, including the German ones. They could tell Hurricanes from Spitfires, Messerschmitt 109s from Messerschmitt 110s. Not that they had seen many

German planes yet, only a few Heinkel He-111s that had got lost. No Messerschmitts.

No one else at school shared their interests. '*Biggles!*' the others said in disgust. They were into Whiteoaks and Rebecca. Even Sidney didn't know as much about aeroplanes as Josie.

Mary lived up by the common in a posh house. Josie didn't like going there very much as you had to take your shoes off inside the front door and wear visitors' slippers. Mary's mother was American. Josie thought her very odd. She was a Christian Scientist, which meant you didn't go to a doctor if something went wrong with you but relied on God to heal you. This resulted in Mary having a bad scar on her face from a bicycle mishap and a crooked arm from not getting it set when she broke it in hockey. But she didn't seem to hold it against her mother, whose prayers had obviously not been very effective. Mary was the school's shining star with her brains and her good behaviour and was obviously set to be head girl next year. Josie never understood why she was her best friend. Was it just Biggles? There must be more than that. When Mary had got another close friend in the sixth form, Netty, Josie had been incredibly hurt and had made a model effigy of Netty to stick pins into, but luckily Netty had been evacuated already – to Canada, which put her well out of the way – and Mary had come back to Josie.

Mary was not interested in boys. She had a crush on a rather glamorous prefect called Diana and loved her passionately. Josie had had a crush on another slightly less glamorous but beautiful prefect called Biddy, but only really to keep up with Mary. But it had lifted her spirits to see beautiful Biddy in prayers every morning; it gave her searching heart something to latch on to, Biddy being more savoury than Sidney, she had to admit. Biddy was the daughter of some high-ranking general and had a fabulous hairstyle. It was straight really, but artfully curled, obviously by more expensive means than curlers in bed, the run-of-the-mill solution to the dire problem of straight hair. Josie's curled, thank God, black and thick. Of course she hated it. Everyone hated what they had and wanted something else. Josie wanted to be blonde, but to peroxide your hair was vulgar. No nice 'gel' did it. Poor Mary had straight mousy-brown hair and lived with it without noticing. She could translate Virgil standing on her head but seemed unaware of what possessed other girls.

'I shall miss you,' she said to Josie.

'You'll meet lots of brains in Oxford, think of that.'

'But not for another year. The sixth form will be terribly thin if no one comes back.'

'Well, if the Germans are here, the school'll be taken over. At least you'll understand what they're talking about. More than I will.'

Mary could talk Latin, French and German. Josie was useless at languages but had had French drummed into her sufficiently for her to manage a conversation. But what good was that now?

'You'll get a job with the Gestapo,' she said to Mary. Mary looked appalled. She had no sense of humour.

Leaving school, which was usually an occasion for celebration, emotional tears at parting and general larks, did not happen that year. Nearly everyone except the exam sitters left in dribs and drabs when the ominous news of the British defeat on the Dunkirk beaches came through on the radio. Josie's father looked up the trains to Auntie Betty's and the date for her departure was fixed. Josie left school without any trumpeting, her teachers shaking her hand and wishing her well but without enthusiasm. She was throwing herself away, they reckoned. She had never been a favourite, only with Matty, the art mistress. They went out to the teashop on Josie's last day, just the two of them, to say goodbye.

Matty lived in Chelsea and was not considering moving out. She hated teaching and painted pictures of cats sitting in windows filled with geraniums, which did not make her enough money to live on. She was getting old, and was ugly and kind, and Josie loved her.

'When I come back in September to start art school, I shall come and see you,' she promised.

'Yes, I hope so. But if the school is evacuated by then, I shan't be going. I shall stay put, whatever. What happens to me is of no consequence. But what happens to you . . . Josie dear, don't get sidetracked. You have a great talent but sometimes I think you take it for granted. You must stay on course. You must work at it, not toss it off. Always strive to do better, that is what it's all about.'

'Yes, I will.'

Josie felt noble and ambitious, fired up by Matty's sincerity, but wondered about striving to be a great artist in Auntie Betty's cottage. It had only just got electricity three months ago, and the lavatory was in a shed outside. But then Van Gogh had lived like that and made great art out of a handful of potatoes, and old boots with mud on them.

'I will work hard, I promise.'

They parted with a handshake, and Matty walked away towards the station to go home to Chelsea. Two Hurricanes flew low overhead, making north. It was hot and the sky was cloudless, criss-crossed in a desultory way by white vapour trails high up. Josie walked home, stopping for five minutes to watch the blacksmith shoeing a horse in his forge just off the high street. She liked this little cul-de-sac of animal industry in amongst the shops; it prompted her to hope she would not prove too ignorant about rural life. Uncle Bert worked on a farm, a far cry from her father's office in Westminster. Did she want to go? She could not work out her feelings exactly: she certainly wasn't excited about it, but the prospect of staying when everyone else was going away was not attractive. It might be a lark, something new, and it would certainly be a great chance to get down to some serious art work as exhorted by Matty. She had never been away from home before, except for holidays with her parents to Westgate or Ilfracombe. She might be homesick. But what for? She was already impatient of her home, with its tight suburban rules, and her boring parents. Even the thought of the Germans coming was more exciting than terrifying. Yet that pitchfork outside the kitchen door . . . however hard she tried, she could not picture it being used. There were some things her imagination did not stretch to. Was it likely, for example, that she might never see her parents again after they parted tomorrow?

Over tea (kippers) her parents acted the same as always, showing no signs of grief at her imminent departure.

'I've packed the things you need,' her mother said. 'You can use my old shopping bag for your own odds and ends, your paints, your knitting and things.'

There was her career, described as 'odds and ends', in an old shopping bag.

'Yes.'

'Your father's going to put you on the train, and Bert said he'd meet you at the other end. It's all arranged.'

Just facts, nothing about feelings. Will you miss me? Josie wondered. Her mother's face was expressionless. But when she went up to bed her mother followed her up and sat on the bed and said, 'I will miss you, Josie. Be a good girl and don't let any boys mess you about. You know what I mean. And be good to your Auntie Betty – don't rub her up the wrong way like you're so

13

fond of doing. It will be hard for her, fitting you in, but with luck it won't be for long.'

'I'm coming back to go to the art school?'

'Yes, God willing. But we none of us know what is going to happen. Write us a letter as often as you can. Maybe your auntie will find you some work to do, to fill in the time. Your cousin Maureen's got a job, I think – a little pocket money wouldn't come amiss. Your father will give you a pound or two tomorrow when you go.'

And then, to Josie's amazement, she put her arms round her and said in a muffled sort of voice, 'We don't seem to get on very well, Josie, but you know I love you really. I want you so much to grow up into a decent girl and do well, so we can be proud of you. Remember that.'

Josie was thrown, embarrassed. She mumbled, 'Yes, Mum, of course. I promise,' and then her mother hurried out of the room, slamming the door.

It was still light, a deep golden sunset flooding her west-facing room. She always had to be in bed by half-past nine and it was hard to go to sleep when the light was still so strong. A blackbird was singing in the lilac tree under her window, and three gardens along someone was mowing the lawn. The familiar noises gave her a sort of ache, inexplicable, soft and sweet, for her happy life, now on the cusp of uncertainty. It was true that she always wanted more, was often dissatisfied, impatient, thrown by circumstances, yet she never really knew what she wanted, was only aware of

14

the wanting. Mixed up. Going away to a new life was exciting, yet from what she knew of it, it was going to be boring. No shops, no London, no Mary, no friends, no books . . . she would die! And yet she wanted to go. Get a job . . . her mother had actually suggested it! Anything might happen. The lawnmower stopped. A dog barked. Otherwise it was silent, the gardens drenched in the last rays of the sun. There was no traffic: no one had cars in their road. The tight-laced little houses had no garages. Wimbledon, a nice suburb for nice families: Josie knew nothing else. Tomorrow it would change.

Chapter Two

The next day Josie travelled into London with her father to catch the train to Auntie Betty's. It seemed to Josie an age since she had been into London and she felt herself absorbing the bustle and familiar smells, the stink of the buses, the lovely burgeoning of the plane trees in the squares, as if she could store them up for her time away. A mere fifty miles, yet she felt she was going to foreign parts. Even being alone with her father – that was a novelty and one she found hard to cope with. Conversation with her monosyllabic father was almost impossible. He had no more idea of what to say to her than she did to him. He was old for a father, nearly sixty, having married late in life. He was twenty years older than her mother and came from a dour Scottish banking family. His uncle had been a famous artist in Scotland and that was why he supported Josie in her desire to go to art school. Her headmistress, saying it was a waste of her talents, had had a sharp rebuff from Mr Marsden, considerably to her surprise. Parents always took her advice. 'It's in her blood,' he said. 'She should do it.' The old girl had had no answer to that. So Josie felt a dogged love for him, although she had no idea what made him tick. Once she had painted a water colour of a horse; it had taken her all day and much sweat, and she was thrilled with the finished product. She showed it proudly to her father, and he said the horse looked like a giraffe: its neck was too long. Josie was outraged and argued angrily against his judgement, at which he had taken the drawing and torn it in two. No word was spoken. Josie had spent the rest of the day hiccuping tears in her bedroom, heartbroken at the destruction of her picture. Her mother had brought her a whipped-cream-walnut, but had been unable to staunch the flow of tears. Josie remembered this now as she sat opposite him in the train, seeing a city gent in a grey suit and a bowler hat, unknowable. She recalled the sharpened pitchfork by the kitchen door. None of it made sense. She felt a sudden lurch of fear at the imminent parting, wondering what on earth was going to happen.

The scenes at the London terminus didn't help, as the platforms were thronged with the soldiers lately landed from Dunkirk. They were no longer the spruce, laughing lads whose pictures had filled the newspapers a few months earlier, but unshaven, dishevelled wrecks in filthy uniforms, some with bandages or with arms in slings, looking as if they had not washed or slept for weeks. They were shepherded kindly, helped, patted on the back, but few smiles came in return. Queues waited outside the Pathé news theatres to see the film of the ongoing evacuation, and the newspaper hoardings blazed headlines about the motley fleet of ships going in to the beaches under heavy fire to take the soldiers off. But the recorded news was as nothing to Josie compared with the look on the face of one man whom she inadvertently stumbled into: he turned on her with an oath, the eyes pits of despair, filled with tears, a nervous tic twitching at his mouth. Another man was supporting him and said, 'Eh up, Teddy, she's not harming you, gently now,' but the man just moaned and wept. Josie felt herself staring. She had never seen a man cry. Her father put his arm round her and pulled her away. 'The poor devils are at the end of their tethers,' he muttered, half moved, half embarrassed by the throng around them. 'What they've suffered – now you see why we want you in a safer place.'

'Why, have we lost the war?'

It seemed obvious, suddenly.

'Not yet.' But there was no conviction in his voice.

'But this is a defeat . . .' The word was on the front of all the newspapers. In her history lessons a defeat had meant a country doomed.

'It'll take more than this. They have to invade us first. Don't worry about it, Josie, we shall win through.'

Josie thought of her Sidney, looking forward to being a soldier. Best he did not come up to Waterloo in the next day or two and see what she was seeing.

They squashed into the tube train going to Liverpool Street and came out into the bleary smoke-filled confines of the mainline station. The same crowd shoved and jostled and swore, and her father, tight-lipped, hurried her through, ticket at the ready.

'This is your train. Let's see if we can find you a seat.'

They were in good time and a seat was found. Her father lifted her suitcase onto the rack and she sat clutching the shopping bag, her heart now pounding with anxiety. Do not cry, she prayed, feeling terribly like it. But why? She wanted to go, didn't she? Her father's moustache was twitching with emotion. He said briefly, 'Be a good girl now. We'll see you soon,' and disappeared abruptly into the throng, no hanging about to wave, no scenes. Lovers were leaning out of the windows entwined in each other's arms. Josie never even saw him go. Suddenly she was alone, squashed into a seat between nine other people, but alone all the same. She felt overcome, exhausted, as if she had been running all day. She leaned back, looking up at the jolly holiday photographs underneath the luggage racks – of children on the beach at Skegness and Great Yarmouth, laughing as if nothing bad could possibly happen. But it *had* happened. Josie had seen it in the soldier's eyes.

She tried to put the doubts out of her mind, but the soldier crying had unhinged her. It was several miles out of London, looking out at the fields of thrusting corn and dazzling woodland holding out its fresh green to the sun, before she started to relax. This was real country, not like Wimbledon Common, and now this was to be her place. She saw now, after crossing London, why her parents wanted her out. Only a few miles, but this scene was untouched by what she had just witnessed. Only fighter planes climbing up into the sun in their familiar V formations disturbed the peace.

The sun was making the carriage uncomfortably warm. Someone opened the window, letting it down a few notches on its leather strap. The breeze fanned Josie's face and calmed her. She was old enough, for heaven's sake, to be travelling alone without feeling panicky, but she scarcely ever had. Certainly she had been going up to London alone for ages, since she was eleven or twelve, but that was home ground. She knew her way around the underground and all the central streets, Kensington and Hyde Park, Victoria and Westminster. But she was a stranger to fields and woods and winding lanes.

The smoke from the engine blobbed across her view, sparks flying up into the sky. The smell came through the window and a speck of soot landed on her nose. Her father told her it was eleven stations to her destination, but the flutter of panic came again when she realized that all the station names had been obliterated, in case of invasion, so she had no idea where she was. An hour and a half, her father had said, but she had no watch anyway. She lost count of the stations: there was a small town and then a little nowhere village, the sort she had pictured she was going to. She started up, plucked up her courage to ask.

'No, dear, not yet. I'll tell you.'

A motherly woman opposite obviously knew her way around, name boards or no name boards. She looked the sort of woman who could use a pitchfork on a German, Josie thought, stout in a mannish way, with beefy, muscled arms. Better than her father. She was comforted for a while, soothed to be in the company of country people who could handle pitchforks. It would be all right, she thought, living in the country. She would like it; she would be safe.

'Here you are, dearie. This is where you want.'

The train was slowing down again. Josie got up and pulled her suitcase off the rack. It wasn't very big and was quite light considering it was filled with most of her summer wardrobe. She was wearing her heaviest thing: her boring navy gabardine raincoat. 'You won't need much stuff up there,' her mother had said darkly, throwing out her two prettiest dresses. Josie had stuffed them back in later.

'Good luck, dear,' said the woman. 'You're well off out of London, the way things are going.'

Josie thanked her and got out. There were few passengers and she soon recognized her Uncle Bert standing by the exit, looking out for her. He was dressed in his farm clothes, no doubt having taken time off to meet her, and greeted her with a shy smile. Like her father he was a man of few words, but he gave off a far easier, friendlier aura, his eyes kindly, his smile ready.

He took her case.

'Eh, pleased to have you, love. Bit of a squash it'll be but you'll not mind that, I hope.'

'No, no.'

She had no conversation. She felt stupid. She followed her uncle out into the station yard to where a horse and trap stood waiting. This was weird. The milk came in a horse and cart at home, but nobody in Wimbledon drove one for transport.

'This is old Freddie from the farm. They let me borrow him when I want, like. He's retired from hard work now. Comes in useful if we want to go anywhere.'

He opened the back door and threw her case in. Josie followed, climbing up by the little step, and sat sideways on, shuffling up to make room for her uncle. He waggled the reins and called, 'Up, Freddie!' and they set off at quite a fast pace, up a street of houses.

'They always go home quicker than they come out, horses,' said Bert.

Josie couldn't think of anything to say at all, but Uncle Bert seemed to take their silence for granted and there was no sense of embarrassment. After her initial anxiety Josie relaxed and started to enjoy this novel mode of travel. The countryside was all rolling fields and large swathes of woodland, and nothing disturbed the peace beyond the sound of the horse's hooves and the occasional squawk of a pheasant. She might have been on a different planet, after London.

22

'Only three miles,' Uncle Bert said at one point, and Josie would have happily had it ten. Down a long hill and at the bottom they pulled up at a crossroads to turn right.

'The airfield's straight on up there, quite busy all of a sudden.They make a row, those fighter planes, I can tell you, but you get used to it. The lads use the village pub so we see a fair bit of them. Funny, but they're only kids, not much older than you.'

'Duxford?'

'No, it's not Duxford. That's further on. This is just for the war, like.'

Freddie flung himself into his collar and pulled them up a hill into a village. Bert let him walk, but when it flattened out the horse trotted again of his own accord. He obviously knew his way for Bert did nothing to guide him as they trotted through the village, mostly a straggle of old cottages with here and there a smarter Georgian mansion and a shop or two. The horse forked left up a lane where the houses petered out and gave way to an avenue of trees leading to a farm. One cottage stood alone on the lane side. It was small with a sagging thatch and little windows like suspicious eyes looking out. Josie recognized it, looking even smaller than she remembered, rather like a tea-cosy, with an embroidered rose rambling over the front door.

'Here we are then.'

He pulled up, and Auntie Betty was there to meet them, taking Josie's case. She was as unlike her sister,

23

Josie's mother, as it was possible for two sisters to be: little and round with bright currant-bun eyes and rosy cheeks, all smiles and bustle.

'Well I never, how you've grown! You're a real young lady now, what a beauty you are! Why, I'd scarcely have known you! Come in now, dear, I've got the dinner ready. Bert'll be back as soon as he's put the horse away. He always comes in for his dinner at midday.'

She prattled on, leading the way round the back of the house where the door stood open. Josie remembered that the front door, leading straight into what was called the parlour, was never used. There was a large garden at the back, cluttered with sheds and outhouses in various states of disrepair, a henhouse and hen-run and – Josie recalled with a lurch of despair – the privy. It was a long walk down an ash path to have a pee; at night one used the chamber pot under the bed. The privy was a two holer, with wooden seats, long polished smooth and shiny by generations of human bottoms. Torn-up sheets of the *Daily Express*, she remembered, hung on a nail. The garden was wholly given over to vegetable growing. There was no lawn or any sign of a deckchair; people didn't sit around in this family.

'Maureen's not back for dinner today. She's out at work. Sometimes she gets back, sometimes not.'

'What does she do?' Josie asked.

'She cleans. She's at the big house today.'

Josie remembered her cousin as dreary. She was the same age as herself, but they hadn't met since they were ten. Anything could have happened. They had to share a bedroom, she discovered. The house only had two. A staircase went up the middle with the four rooms – two up, two down – equally divided. Downstairs were the parlour (rarely used) and the living room and kitchen combined. A scullery was tacked on the back where a tin bath hung on the door, which had to be filled by buckets of hot water taken from the kitchen range. Josie remembered that baths here were weekly affairs, although Bert took more when he was muck-spreading or cleaning out the pigsties. When it was cold in the winter she remembered the tin bath had been brought in from the scullery and put by the fire and she had enjoyed that. The scullery was cold. They had visited at Christmas sometimes, but she knew her father didn't like it here, a fish out of water with his rustic relations. Her mother had insisted. She didn't like it either but thought it necessary, to 'keep in touch'. 'It's family, Joe,' she had said. No answer. Joe had never kept in touch with his family and Josie had never met the few cousins on his side. They sent Christmas cards, that's all.

Privy, tin bath and all, she decided quite soon that she liked it. There was an unfamiliar sense of certainty, of order, of irrevocability, that she hadn't felt in Wimbledon. It was earthy, real. Meeting an invader with a pitchfork made far more sense out here, where people knew how to use a pitchfork. Country people were stalwart, thick, steady. The difference was a novelty; perhaps after a while it would become boring.

She did not know. There was so much to learn initially: about the crops that surrounded them, the farm cycle, Auntie Betty's mangle, bread-making, the village hierarchy, the way Maureen's mind worked. Lots to draw: the hens, Freddie, cows, woods, the distant view of the big house, the landscape. She was given jobs: shopping, weeding, cleaning out the henhouse, dusting, cleaning the windows, mowing the grass – all things that she would have done for her mother with loathing, but which she did here with a mindless enjoyment, humming the new songs they heard on the wireless every night. Uncle Bert listened to the wireless when he came home; it was on all the time. He had his tea, worked for an hour on the vegetable garden, then came in, turned the knob, settled in his chair and listened to the news, Churchill's speeches, Arthur Askey's jokes, Harry Hall's dance band and dire warnings about careless talk in public, using too much bathwater ('What a hope!') and showing lights in the dark. He usually fell asleep, but the radio played on.

'I do the big house Tuesdays, Wednesdays and Fridays and old Mrs Sylvester Mondays and Thursdays. At the weekend there's the pub, washing up and stuff. I'm not allowed in the bar – I'm too young – but Albert doesn't bother very much. If you want a job, I could get you in there. If you want, that is.'

Did she want? A pub! What would her headmistress say!

Josie giggled.

'Is it just old farmers in there? Anyone interesting?'

'Gorgeous young men?' Maureen giggled too. 'No. Only Jumbo.'

'Who's Jumbo?'

'Jumbo lives at the big house. He's only got one leg.'

'What happened to the other one?'

'It came off in a motorcycle accident. Well, afterwards, I mean. It was amputated.'

'How old is he?'

'Eighteenish.'

Josie was reminded of Sidney, whom she had almost forgotten. Of course he hadn't come to see her, the rat.

Maureen said, 'Jumbo's – well, you know – different. Coming from the big house. He's a fish out of water. He was never here before his accident. He was either at boarding school, or away in the holidays – climbing, skiing, whatever. What rich people do. Now he's stuck. At least, until he gets a new leg. And now, with all the soldiers, that's not going to happen in a hurry.'

'Blimey, how awful!'

'He doesn't talk to me. Well, only hullo. I'm only the maid, you see.'

'Are they nice, at the big house?'

'They're all right.'

Maureen, Josie had discovered, was not quite so dreary as she remembered. She was a plain girl with straight mousy hair which she had to put in curlers every night, a bit spotty, moon-faced, with large,

27

slightly bulging grey eyes. She had no ambition, little education and seemed perfectly contented with her lot. Josie envied her her lack of uncertainty, of enquiry. She went to the cinema on Saturday nights, taking the bus into town with her boyfriend Tom, who worked with Bert on the farm. On Friday nights they went to a dance. Maureen tried to persuade Josie to come to the dances but Josie refused. She hated dances, standing against the wall waiting for some nervous, pawing boy to invite her and then finding their great feet always in the way, stumbling and apologizing. She would sit on the bed in their room watching Maureen applying her Tangee lipstick and trying to revive her flagging curls with a hot iron. The whole room smelled of burning hair and cheap talcum powder.

'Honestly, you'd like it. You might meet someone nice.'

Josie felt stuck-up refusing, but she didn't want a country clod for a boyfriend.

'I suppose you went to posh sort of dances in Wimbledon.'

'No. Only school things. And I never liked them. I'm no good at dancing.'

They had had lessons after school and she knew all the steps, but mostly she had danced as the man, there being no males in the class. She liked the lessons, but didn't like the real thing. It was confusing dancing backwards when you were used to being the man.

'Oh, it's lovely. The last waltz . . .' Maureen looked

dreamy. Josie supposed she was in love. Tom was a slender, blond lad of few words, awaiting call-up. Josie didn't fancy him. She didn't miss Sidney; she hadn't loved him, only found the idea of loving someone intriguing. If she was to go to art school in September she knew she must use this summer to work, not gallivant off to find boyfriends who would distract her. She was full of good intentions. When she had no more chores to do around the house she went out with her sketchbook and paints to work. The countryside at the beginning of June was so beautiful, but could she paint it without it looking cheap and chocolate-boxy? Paint it like Turner or Gainsborough? She was better at live things; trees were terribly difficult. But Matty had said practise. 'Even when you do a bad drawing, you learn something. Perseverance is everything. It's not a spare-time job, art.'

Josie decided to go across the fields to a lake that lay on the far side of the village. It was surrounded by trees except for one place where what had once been a lawn sloped up from the bank to the remains of an old house. Sometimes cows grazed here now; occasionally there was an old man fishing. But mostly it was deserted save for a family of swans and numerous coots and moorhens. Josie thought it very romantic, and could see in her imagination the house in its heyday, with Edwardian ladies on the lawn, butlers bringing out the tea. The house was now just a shell, with ivy growing up the inside walls. Somehow it was more beautiful as a ruin than if it had been full of life: its tranquillity in its circlet of woodland attracted Josie. She had never known a place so peaceful. It was hard, in fact, to work when she had unpacked her shopping bag and spread her old rug out on the grass and arranged her sketchbook and paints . . . she needed shade over her paper, but liked to feel the sun on her bare arms. She shuffled about to get it right like an old dog in its basket, arranging and rearranging. Then she wanted to just sit and look and drink it in, not work. Enjoy it. She was almost deliriously happy, aware of her fortune. People were being bombed to bits not far away; the fighter planes had gone out with a roar when she had left the house and would be back before long to refuel and wait for the next alarm, yet this place was a world separate, untouched. The only sound was of birdsong, of thrushes in the woods and ducks muttering from the lake, and the humming of passing bees searching out the clover in the grass. Somewhere not far away Maureen was cleaning the bathroom, tipping Harpic down the lavatory, hoovering the stairs, and here she was leaning against a tree on her rug, drinking in beauty, about to capture it in her sketchbook. She was lucky!

She started to work. Soon she was lost in it, screwing up her eyes to set out the proportions on the page, then going straight to paint. She was always too impatient to make a careful initial drawing, even when she found time after time that, if she had spent longer looking at the start, she would have avoided the tangle that always happened later. Quite soon she could see that the lawn was wrong in proportion to the height of the house, but she had already sploshed in the dark swags of ivy and could not move the house. If she got the lawn right, there would be no room for the lake at the bottom. This was when she started inventing. She didn't think Turner ever got in this sort of muddle. She pulled another page out and added it to the underneath, to be glued on later. Her drawings nearly always went off the page. She hoped it was a sign of magnanimity, generosity, not just carelessness.

Intent as she was, when a voice hailed her she jumped so violently that she all but knocked her jam jar of water over. She grabbed it, and a large dollop of green paint flew off her brush onto the white wall of the house.

'Oh damn!'

She put her rag over it – disaster . . . she would never get it out!

'Oh dear, was that my fault? Sorry.'

The voice was amiable, sorry but not distraught. Laughing a bit. What sort of an idiot was this intruder seeing, scratching at this bad drawing? Josie felt herself going scarlet. The figure was standing against the sun, so that all she could see was a silhouette, lithe, slender, the flash of a smile. He leaned on crutches and had only one leg so she knew who it was immediately.

'Jumbo!'

Because of the name she had pictured a large

31

lumbering youth, so the surprise showed in her voice. Her flash of annoyance faded: how could she but feel a surge of pleasure at the appearance of this undeniably attractive young man smiling at her in the sunshine? But she was embarrassed and confused, not experienced enough to say all the right things, only to stammer an apology for her flash of anger. He had the easy confidence of the public schoolboy, the rich kid. She recognized it, and felt inadequate.

'I've never met anyone here,' he said. 'I got a surprise too, seeing you. How do you know I'm Jumbo?'

'My cousin told me about you. She works in your house; she cleans. Maureen.'

'Ah, you're the evacuee, I know. You see, everyone knows everything round here. We must be careful in case there are spies around. Careless talk costs lives.' He laughed. 'What did she say about me? Nice things?'

'Well, about the leg, that's all. And you're waiting for a false one and it might take a long time.'

'Yes, that's true unfortunately. But at least I'm still alive. One has to look on the bright side.' But even as he said this his bright side darkened momentarily and Josie saw in a flash how it was for an eighteen-year-old who had lived for skiing and climbing to lose a leg. His face was very expressive, sun and shadow chasing.

'At least you won't get called up.' Josie meant this to comfort, but saw at once that she had got it wrong.

'No. I was going into the air force like my brother. He's a fighter pilot. That's what I wanted.'

Darkness descended again, not helped by the sudden roar of a Hurricane zooming in to land up on the hill, as if laughing at the boy's ruined ambition.

'Look, if you want to get on with your painting, I won't stop you,' he said abruptly. 'I know how it is – my mother paints. She gets mad if you interrupt her.'

'No, it doesn't matter.'

But he had swung away, twirling round on his crutches. He was extraordinarily agile.

'I'll see you again. I come here nearly every day, keeping fit. I go for miles.' He laughed then and went bounding up the slope towards the house, disappearing round the side. He went quicker on crutches than an ordinary person could walk. Josie stared after him, bemused. Having left her to her work, he had completely eclipsed the problems of her watercolour, an insipid thing by comparison with his beguiling presence. Her thoughts were now all over the place.

She pushed the drawing away and leaned back against her tree-trunk. The sun was getting warmer by the minute and she felt equally warmed by her surprising visitor. She relaxed and let her calm come back, turning her face into the sun. How lucky she was – to have two legs, to be here, to have no worries! Only her art. She looked at the drawing again and saw that it wasn't bad – good enough to go on with. She knew that if she completed a good piece of work it made her day. She would keep going back to look at it afterwards, with pleasure. So she soon started work again, and painted steadily for a couple of hours and was pleased at the end of it to see that she had captured the curious, romantic character of the rotting house with its lawn and lake, and the white swans in the foreground.

'What is the story of that ruined house by the lake?' she asked Auntie Betty when she got home.

'The manor? Oh, it belonged to an old family – posh folks, you know – but they died out. The last two sons were killed in the war – the last war, that is – and when the old people died there was no one left. And of course there was a depression then in farming, in the country, no money. Nobody wanted a place like that, so far from anywhere. So it just went to rack and ruin.'

'I met that boy Jumbo.'

'Oh, poor Jumbo, yes – he covers miles on those crutches. He was a real athlete before, ran for his school and all that, always on the go. Poor lad, what a tragedy! But I suppose it might save him from being killed. His brother's a fighter pilot and Jumbo was going to follow him. He was already in the air force, just starting his training, when it happened. His poor mother – having them both fighter pilots! In her heart I think she's probably relieved the way it turned out.'

'That's dreadful!'

'Yes, it is. But think of it. Her oldest boy, Chris – he's been in France since last September. He was in the air force before the war and already trained when the

34

Germans overran France. They were sent over to try and stop the Luftwaffe. I think he was shot down twice, captured once and escaped, and I hear he's been awarded the DFC. He's back now, stationed somewhere down in Sussex. That's enough for a mother to worry about, without having two of them!'

Josie was pleased with her sketch, as she glued the extra page on the bottom of it. It wasn't brilliant but it had captured, somehow, the dreamy isolation of the forgotten house. The atmosphere was right. How did one paint an atmosphere? It warmed her, to think that she was going to be a success with her art. She would work very hard and not be distracted, as Matty had instructed her. Not be led astray.

Chapter Three

Jumbo swung up through the woods, disturbed by his surprising encounter. In all his ramblings he rarely met anyone save a farmhand or gamekeeper, and he had never met anyone before in the manor grounds. The old 'PRIVATE' signs had long rotted away and even the locals weren't sure any longer who owned the place. He and Chris had made camps in the ruins once, and lit fires, but now the village children preferred to play in some old army camp ruins on the other side of the village from where they could spy on the aeroplanes.

Jumbo thought that, when he was old and successful, he would buy this place and bring it back to life. Well, he had thought that once but now, with one leg, being successful wasn't a certainty. Losing his leg had changed his life – you could say that again! Until recently he had come to this quiet place to rant and rave and even to cry, knowing there were only the swans to listen, the thrushes to take fright. At home, at school, one took these things on the chin, however ghastly. One's parents stiffened if emotion was in the air. 'Take it like a man,' his father had said during his first visit to the hospital. And Jumbo was forced to act up to it, for his father had been blinded in the last war. He had learned to cope, to read Braille, to travel alone, to work. What was a leg compared to that? Jumbo knew he had something to live up to. But when he thought of the mountains he cried. It was only the example of the poet Geoffrey Winthrop Young that could revive his spirit: a mountaineer who had lost a leg in the war and had learned to climb again with his prosthetic limb. Jumbo had climbed with his brother every long school holiday: in Scotland, in Wales, then in the Alps. They had planned the Himalayas, lying in bed with their books of Everest expeditions.

'I have not lost the magic of long days;
I live them still.
Still am I master of the starry ways,
And freeman of the hill.
Shattered my glass, ere half the sands had run,
I hold the heights, I hold the heights I won.'

Jumbo quoted it sternly. But he had lost his leg at seventeen. Much less than half his sands had run; a mere bloody quarter, if that. 'It's not fair!' he cried out in the serene woodland of the old manor, holding on as best he could. But sometimes he thrashed in the grass, rolling and sobbing. Then he was ashamed and would stumble down to the lake and shout at the swans. Had his father ever screamed at the injustice, dry old stick that he was? If he had, he would never admit to it, just as he, Jumbo, never would either.

'Oh, he's taken it very well. He's managing – very brave,' his mother would tell the relatives.

He would smile like an idiot. Nothing to it, old chap. Hop along, you know. No problem. The public face.

Lucky, in fact, that he had a happy, optimistic nature, else he would have gone round the bend with frustration. He had experienced depression, and never wanted that again. But people lived with depression, even given they had no reason; they had all their limbs, their sight. He was better equipped than them. Chris had cheered him: 'Get a leg as soon as you can. They're as good as the real thing. There's pilots with false legs.' Jumbo watched for the post every day, knowing he was on a waiting list. But how long, for God's sake, now the Dunkirk men were streaming in? It felt like for ever. They had promised before September. Well, it was June now. But in a life-time three months was not much.

God, what if he had been indulging in his hysterics when that girl Josie had been there? He would have died of shame. But he kicked himself for not staying longer to chat – what a missed opportunity! It had been such a surprise, swinging down the edge of the lawn and almost falling over this fawnlike creature nes-tled in the grass. Dappled with sunlight, her face turned up with huge startled eyes meeting his, she was stamped emphatically in his visual memory. Like a photograph. She was lovely. He could not stop thinking about her.

His home, Nightingales, stood at the end of a long drive on the airfield side of the village. It was well-wrapped in trees and shrubberies, hidden from the road, an early Victorian pile of considerable grandeur but slightly run down. Jumbo's parents were not much concerned with homemaking; their interests lay elsewhere. His father, Lieutenant Colonel Patterson, was chauffeured up to the War Office in London most days, or was otherwise shut in his office, and his mother Marjorie was either painting horse portraits in her studio or out of sight down in the stables with her brood mares and hunters. To run the house they employed minimum staff: a gardener called Percy, Maureen the cleaning girl and Tilly, once Marjorie's nanny, who cooked and generally organized the house.

Neither Jumbo nor his brother Chris had taken to horses, much to their mother's grief, but they liked the dogs she seemed to collect. Zulu, a chunky English springer, ran joyously to meet Jumbo as he hopped up the drive, his tail twirling like a windmill.

'Where were you when I set out this morning, then? You missed your swim in the lake.'

Just as well, Jumbo thought to himself, imagining the damage the wet dog would have done to the girl's drawing. God, he was hungry! What was for lunch? He crutched his way into the kitchen, a great gaunt room with an old-fashioned kitchen range taking up most of

39

one side – mostly unused and never lit in the summer – and a conglomeration of deep sinks and washing boilers under the window. The floor was flagged and cold. The table in the middle was heaped with horse tack waiting to be cleaned; no sign of lunch.

'I'm starving!'

His mother said, 'There's nothing till one o'clock. Tilly's gone to the village. Make yourself some toast.'

She looked just like her kitchen, gaunt and spare, undecorated. She wore breeches and a frayed shirt, her greying hair scraped back, thin and hard as a whippet. Jumbo knew that, dressed up, she was stunning, with her aristocratic, high cheekbones and arrow-straight nose, scornful eyes and arrogant posture, but as a mother she wasn't even in the ratings, too angular for cuddles, hopeless for confidences, blank to childish thinking. She was soaping her saddle, standing at the table.

'Has the post been?' Jumbo asked, always hopeful for a letter telling him he was summoned to the leg place.

'Nothing for you. Not especially, that is, but I suppose you're included in ours – an invitation to the palace when Chris gets his medal. That'll be a nice day out.'

'To the palace? Blimey! I thought the king went and doled them out on site.'

'Yes, I thought so too. But it's nice to be invited.'

'Poor old Chris! He'll hate it. Funny when you think he nearly got bowler-hatted for flying under Tower Bridge that time. And now, for being just as brave, he gets a medal instead.'

'Times change. I asked him what he got his medal

for but he said, God knows, why me? He said they should all get one, or not at all. But I must say his time in France has changed him. He's not the boy he was. Why does he never come home?'

'There's nothing here for him,' Jumbo said, without tact.

His mother gave him an angry glance which, noticing, he parried with: 'They stick together on leave. Spend their time living it up, getting drunk. It's not just Chris.'

He understood, even if his mother didn't. They never came home before, if she remembered. It suited her to send them away to boarding school, and it suited them to live it up away from home in the holidays – mostly in the mountains, or sailing, drinking, getting into trouble. His leg had stopped him, and Chris's job had stopped *him*. It was different now. She ought to realize. Chris spoke to him, he didn't speak to his parents. He was in his own, taut little closed-shop world, dicing with death, and there was no time for outside it, nor inclination.

'I met a girl just now – Maureen's cousin, the evacuee. She's stunning. Have you seen her?'

'Not that I know of. She's at the farm cottage, I take it, with Maureen's parents. Must be a tight fit, that little place.'

'Just think, we could take dozens of evacuees here.'

His mother visibly shuddered. 'God forbid! Thank goodness this isn't an area for it, not far away enough. I haven't been asked.'

'What if you were?'

41

'I'd fight tooth and nail! Some officers from the airfield if the worst came to the worst, but little snotty kids – never!'

Jumbo laughed. 'Well, you can take this kid! She's lovely. And she paints – that was what she was doing, sketching the old manor.'

'How nice.'

Deprecating. Jumbo knew how his mother's eyes would rake the girl if he brought her home. The hawk eyes that probed her horse 'sitters' and magically brought them to life on the canvas would terrify her. Chris, for whom girls fell off the trees, never brought his girls home. They were nearly always the sort his mother would abhor – common, in a word. And these girls who so adored his brother never had eyes for him, save as a shoulder to weep on when they were shrugged off, as always happened. They liked him but did not fall for him as they did for Chris. He had never much bothered about that before, but now – presumably because he had nothing else to do – he found his thoughts coming back to this cousin of Maureen's all the time. He asked Maureen about her.

'Is she with you for long?'

'Until September, when she's supposed to go to art school back home. If nothing goes wrong, that is. If the jerries don't come.'

Funny they were cousins, this dumpy, flat-faced maid and the little jewel in the woods. Or was she a jewel? He was now hallucinating, spurred by boredom. She was probably as boring as hell. He must find out.

Chapter Four

Josie pretended she wanted to improve on her drawing of the manor. That was her reason for going back. But in her heart she knew she wanted to meet Jumbo again. It had been so brief before; she had scarcely managed to take him in before he had gone hopping back up the hill like one of the big grey herons that fished in the rushes. Against the sun, the light had made a halo out of his fair, untidy hair and his features had flickered in the dappled sunlight, alert, mocking – now, luring her back. Like a fly for a fish, she thought, attracted, curious, hopeful.

He looked a better prospect than Sidney Buck, who – the rat – had never been seen nor heard of again. Josie was tired of hearing Maureen prattling on about Tom; she wanted a boyfriend too. Maureen, rumbling Josie's curiosity, said, 'Cor, you don't want one of those – quality . . . they'd drive you potty with their funny ways.'

'What do you mean?'

'They're not like us. They don't talk, house falling

43

apart, full of mice, cold as charity, but they eat off plates that Tilly says are worth a hundred quid a throw – that's what she told me when I was washing up once. I put it down and refused to wash up ever again – rather get the sack. She laughed. She says the missus wouldn't notice. But in the stables, if Percy doesn't wash the feed buckets spotless after every feed she goes absolutely nutty. They're all raving mad up there.'

'What, Jumbo too?'

'No, he's all right. Doesn't say much. He's so fed up, stuck with his leg, waiting. He doesn't moan though.'

She was waiting too, Josie realized, filling in time. Waiting to see what was going to happen. They could wait together. She went back to draw the old manor, and on the second day they met again.

Josie was down by the lake, out in the open where he would find her. He came down across the lawn. There was no shock this time, both acknowleging that they had intended to meet, but without saying so. All the same, Josie felt her colour rising as he approached and her pulse beating faster. The calculated way of it embarrassed her. But she wanted it. Did he feel the same?

Yes, but she could tell he was uncertain.

'I'm not disturbing you?'

'No. I haven't really started yet. Just looking.'

'Can I stay a little? I generally rest up here a bit. My arms get tired.'

'No, stay. Fine.'

He sank down in the grass, throwing the crutches to one side. He was lanky and very agile. His amputated leg stopped above the knee, the trouser leg roughly amputated to match and sewn up with large, untidy stitches, probably by himself, Josie thought, as according to Maureen his mother wasn't very motherly. He had a friendly, boyish face, slightly freckled, fair hair and hazel eyes. He could have been a young Biggles, with that clean-cut air and direct look. There was no subtlety in his approach.

'I've never seen any girls round here before. I didn't stop to introduce myself before – I got a bit of a fright, nearly falling over you. So I thought I'd come and look for you again. And hey presto, here you are.' He grinned.

'Why are you called Jumbo? You don't look like one.'

'I've no idea. I think my brother called me Jumbo when we were little and it stuck. It's better than my real name, which I keep quiet about, so he did me a service. We did everything together, until this business. I was going into the air force too, had applied and been accepted, was just starting, in fact, been in a few weeks. So you can see I'm a bit 'fed up' just now.'

Josie rather thought 'fed up' was an understatement. Maureen said they were all mad up there, of course.

'I would have screamed and cried for ages! I'd have gone crazy.'

Jumbo said, 'It doesn't get you anywhere.'

'Yes, well, it's how you feel.'

45

'It's not always best to give way to how you feel.'

True, that's what she was taught too. 'No, I know. But—' She shrugged. That's how it was. 'It would have been better if you hadn't planned what you were going to do. A lot of blokes would have been quite glad to have an excuse not to be called up.'

'Like shooting yourself in the foot. I think that's what they did sometimes, in the last war, to go home. But most of them today are dying to join up, aren't they?'

Josie recalled the soldiers she had seen at Waterloo and Liverpool Street, and wasn't so sure.

'They all were at school, anyway,' Jumbo said. 'Couldn't wait. Me too. But later when I've got a false leg I'm going to try again. Chris says it's possible, although he may be just saying that to kid me along. I don't know. I can't sit at a desk all my life, I know I can't.'

'How old is Chris?' Josie thought quite a lot older but Jumbo said, 'Nearly twenty. He was already trained when war started and was sent to France. I think they had a tough time out there. He's stationed in Sussex now. He's only been home the once, after France. He slept all the time. Now he's at Tangmere, on the coast. I suppose, with luck, he might get stationed here but it's probably unlikely.'

'What does he fly? A Spitfire?'

'No. A Hurricane.'

'Is he like you?'

'No, he's dark and handsome and brave, nothing

46

like me at all. I've always just tagged along. We did everything together, before. This time last year he had a long leave and we went to the Alps and climbed. It was fantastic, the best thing I've ever done. We climbed the Matterhorn, which is tough but not difficult, then we went to Chamonix and played about on the Needles. We did some quite difficult ones – the Dru, the Walker Spur . . . it was fantastic and we said then, it was just a beginning, we would do them all, even the Eiger, and later go to the Himalayas. Afterwards we got a couple of weekends in Scotland – great weekends – but he couldn't get any more time off, and then that was it. The war came, this happened, it's all pie in the sky now. I sometimes think it would be better if it had never happened, and then I wouldn't know what I was missing.'

'Oh no, you mustn't say that! You proved you can do it – how would you ever know otherwise? You got it in, didn't you?'

'Well, I suppose. Depends how you look at it. I suppose I can get up the easy ones eventually, get up there and look – oh, you can't believe how wonderful it is, to bivouac and wake in the dawn and see the sun coming to touch the tops, light them up one by one – it's magical. I often think Chris can see that in his plane – he says sometimes up there you can't believe how beautiful it is. My father is blind, you know. So that is a hundred times worse. Think of it. I tell myself that.'

'Oh yes. That must be dreadful.'

'I'm sorry. I didn't mean to spill all this out. It's a beautiful morning – every day, such a fantastic summer. I could be dead, after all. It's nice meeting you. Have you got a boyfriend at home?'

'No, well, perhaps. I had one. But he's not been to see me, not even written, so I don't think I've got one now. I don't care. He was only a stupid boy—' She was just about to add 'on a motorbike' but bit the words off just in time. 'Quite nice but nothing special,' she finished lamely.

'I thought you'd have dozens.'

'Oh no! I'm very backward.'

'I'm backward too. Never thought of girls. Chris has dozens. Not that he seems to care about them, that I've noticed. He only carries a photo of his old dog in his wallet.'

Josie giggled. 'That's nice. I like dogs.'

He wanted to know about her, so she told him about her boring non-life-story in Wimbledon and how she wanted to go to art school. It occurred to her how very undramatic her life was: it took less than a minute to tell what had occurred in her sixteen years. Was that normal? She didn't know.

'Really boring,' she excused herself.

'Nothing much happens till you leave school,' Jumbo said equably. 'Would you like to go to the pictures tonight? We can go on the bus. Get fish and chips first, if you like. Do you fancy it?'

'Oh yes, I do. Maureen goes with her Tom every weekend. I can find out what's on. Perhaps it's a

Deanna Durban film – I love her.'

'Hmm. Give me George Formby any day of the week. We can argue about it when we get there. There's three cinemas. The bus goes at six-thirty from the pub, so we could meet up there.'

'Yes, all right.'

'I'll leave you to draw. Never let it be said I came between you and your career. I wish I could draw. I can't do anything – sing, dance, play the violin, nothing.'

Josie laughed. 'What does it matter? One day you'll do great things!'

She thought that, with his courage and optimism, this could well be true and spoke with conviction, but he laughed and said, 'Flattery will get you nowhere. I'll see you tonight.'

He rolled over, reached for his crutches, and went bounding away up the lawn to disappear through the ruins of the house.

Josie knew she must start work but her work ethic seemed to be shattered. All she could see as she searched for her landscape was the amused face of the boy from Nightingales, gazing at her with appreciative eyes. He was lovely, one leg or two, handsome and engaging, brave and funny. What more could one ask? She had not expected the meeting to be so productive: he didn't waste time. She hoped he wouldn't spoil it. There was all the summer, after all.

Chapter Five

The film was a Ginger Rogers and Fred Astaire. Josie loved them and Jumbo said he could bear it, just. He never could dance anyway, even when he had two legs.

'Chris tried to teach me. He's wizard. But I'm useless. I hope you don't want to go dancing?'

'No, not really.'

She'd never been to a dance with a boy, only with other girls when you had to sit in a row against the wall waiting for a boy to come and ask you to dance, which was totally humiliating. You chatted vigorously with your friends, pretending your conversation was enthralling and that that was all you were there for, but all the time you were praying, *praying* for a boy to approach you, however spotty or deformed he might be. Smart girls eyed the smart boys and winked, but Josie was unable to do that. She just wanted to die.

'No. I don't like dancing. Maureen keeps trying to make me go, but I don't want to.'

'Thank goodness. We'll stick with the cinema and fish and chips. You're very obliging.'

They met at the bus stop outside the pub in the late afternoon. Josie had got the OK from Auntie Betty. 'Jumbo from Nightingales? The Patterson boy? My word, you're flying high! His father's some sort of a general, I believe. And the mother – she's no time of day for anybody unless they're on a horse.'

'Well, he's very nice.'

'Yes, so I believe, the poor lad. And the brother too, what a pair! You might find yourself out of your depth there, my girl. You be careful.'

Josie knew all this from Maureen, but to her Jumbo seemed very down-to-earth and on her level. He had no airs and graces. He came hopping up in good time and they sat on the pub wall waiting for the bus. Josie had been nervous about meeting him again, and felt her blood racing as he came into view and the colour crashing up into her cheeks. This was her first real date ever, she thought, dismissing the casual unannounced meetings that Sidney had considered courting, and it seemed a terribly important landmark in her life. She could not believe her luck in finding someone as congenial as Jumbo. And even though, as he said, he had never dated girls before, his background gave him a practised amiability with someone still virtually a stranger. No blushing and fumbling and embarrassment in his greeting, nor hesitancy in the way he handed her politely into the bus.

'How goes it, Jumbo?' The bus driver winked, having given Josie a quick, appraising stare. 'Got word about your leg yet?'

'No, just a rough suggestion – about September. Here's hoping.'

'You'll be in the air force yet.'

'I hope so.'

He had the same easy manner with everyone, seeming much older than his seventeen years. Confidence: Josie put it down to the public school influence. Poor Sidney couldn't compete, even if he had taught her . . . well, she had learned a few things from Sidney . . . she wished she didn't blush so. She could feel the heat rising again in her cheeks.

They bought fish and chips and ate them out of the newspaper, sitting on a street bench. The town, such as it was, was ancient and cramped, very pretty. There was scarcely any traffic, since petrol had been stopped save for priorities.

'Not that there ever was,' Jumbo said. 'Nothing ever happens here, not until you get near Cambridge. Cambridge is a smashing place. Now I'm so stuck, it's pretty confining living where we do. When I get my leg, I'll be off. London probably.'

'I'm going back in September.'

They went into the cinema. The B film was awful, as usual, and the Pathé newsreel before the big film was disturbing. It was fixed on Hitler's preparation for an invasion. Goering, the head of the Luftwaffe, was said to be favouring a 'softening-up' initiative by bombing all the airfields round London to put the air force out of action.

'Looks like you're evacuated to the wrong place,

with our airfield just across the way,' Jumbo whispered to Josie.

Josie hoped her mother wasn't watching this film. She went to the cinema most weeks, so she probably was. Josie didn't want to go home, not now.

The commentator said in his excited voice: 'Hitler has ordered the Luftwaffe to overcome the British air force with all means at its disposal and in the shortest time possible.'

'Blimey, poor old Chris,' said Jumbo.

'And a paramount blow to British feelings: the French government under Marshall Pétain has released its captured German pilots back to Germany. This in spite of strong British representation to bring them to Britain as prisoners of war.'

'Bloody hell, to go on fighting our lot! The man's a criminal!' Jumbo hissed.

A few minutes later Fred Astaire and Ginger Rogers were swirling across the screen and the war could have been on another planet. But Josie's confidence in the future was dented, and the sharp visual memory of the Dunkirk soldiers came back to her. That was defeat. There was no denying the news was very bad.

It seemed strange to think of it when they came out. It was still light, the end of a perfect summer day, the midges biting, the last swallows going to nest. When they got off the bus Jumbo walked her back home, swinging slowly on the crutches.

'God, if only I could be a part of it! I was going to be such an ace pilot, just like Chris. And what if he gets killed? They're up against it, totally outnumbered, and if they fail old Hitler'll be here before Christmas. I can't believe it! I'd give anything to be with Chris now, like we'd planned. I'd give my right arm!' He laughed angrily. 'I've already given my right leg.'

'Do you think it really will happen?'

'It will if we don't beat them in the air. Nothing to stop them then.'

Those soldiers hadn't stopped them, after all. And what had Churchill said on the wireless? 'We shall defend our island, whatever the cost may be. We shall fight on the beaches, we shall fight on the landing grounds; we shall fight in the fields and in the streets, we shall fight in the hills; we shall never surrender.' The juicy, stentorian tones of his voice over the crackly wireless had moved her, had moved them all, even Uncle Bert.

'By gum, he's right. That's what we'll do, we'll beat the buggers.'

'Language, Bert!' from Auntie Betty. And then, 'Yes, the buggers.'

Cows were grazing peacefully over the hedge, their soft scent mingling with the evening dew smell, tails twitching against the midges. Beyond them a belt of trees hid the aerodrome from view. But even as they struck up the lane a couple of Hurricanes came in to land, fast and low from the south. The raucous noise of their engines was now as familiar as the bluetits' twittering in the thatch. Josie scarcely noticed them any longer, but Jumbo paused to watch.

54

'Could be Chris,' he murmured. 'Maybe he'll be based here one day. They move 'em around all the time.'

And in his choked voice Josie heard the longing that he so successfully hid most of the time, to be where he should have been, flying with his brother. They stood in the deep twilight of high summer, looking at the apparently eternal pastoral scene of peaceful meadows and hearing the rhythmic chewing of the cows over the hedge, and both were thinking of what they had heard in the cinema, the threat to destroy it all.

'Chris told me, when he was on leave, that they were lying about on the edge of the airfield in France, waiting to be scrambled, and nearby there was a man and his son harrowing a field with two pairs of horses, and all of a sudden a German bomber appeared out of the blue and dropped a stick of bombs. He missed everything on the airfield but blew the peasants and the horses to bits. He said it made them sick. Worse than if it had been them. It made no sense.'

They stood watching the cows. The first stars were faintly speckling the cloudless sky. It was very hard to picture death and destruction in such a setting, to take in the fact that the threat was so real. Better to think of Fred Astaire's astonishing feet. Josie was nervous of the emotion in Jumbo's voice and did not know what to say. But to her relief he quickly jerked himself out of it, saying, 'I suppose you're a refugee of sorts. Lucky you came my way!'

Josie wondered if, had he a hand to spare, he might have held hers. But she was aware of a pleasant feeling between them as they continued up the lane, the feeling she had had before of being with a congenial spirit. When they got to the cottage gate he said, 'When shall I see you again? Nice and soon, I hope?'

'Yes.'

'Tomorrow?'

'Yes.'

'I'll meet you by the lake. I'll bring a book and read, and you can draw. Is that OK?'

'Yes.'

'Make the most of it. Before the Germans get us.'

'Yes.'

He hopped away. Josie stood watching him, feeling warm with their friendship, glad that he had not spoiled it with the fumbling she associated with Sidney. She didn't want that. She liked being Jumbo's friend. She wanted to stay in that undemanding state, not tumbled into the Sidney sort of thing, where it was nothing about friendship. She realized how lonely she was here, since she had been away from all her school friends. If they hadn't all been scattered away like herself she would be longing to be back home by now. Maureen was useless as a friend, only talking about Tom and make-up, and there was no one else. Auntie Betty thought she should get a job, get out and about. She had said so several times.

'Even in the pub, with Maureen. You're too young for the bar, but there's plenty of life there in the evenings when the boys come up. You could help in the back, washing up, cleaning, see a bit of life.'

Jumbo went to the pub in the evenings. Maybe the landlord would let her sit with an orange juice. There was nowhere else to go. Washing up with Maureen did not hold a great appeal. But it was true that, now the novelty of country life was wearing off, she was getting bored. Her work, without stimulus from outside, was not fulfilling her as she had hoped. Auntie Betty was scornful. 'It's no thing for a girl like you, spending all day over a bit of paper. What's it for?'

'What's it for!'

Josie could not begin to answer. What was anything for? To get a job one day, like Matty? Matty hated teaching. She painted pictures she could not sell, but never gave up. Josie had done enough to know how it felt, when the work came out well. It was what she wanted to do. But it was hard now, she realized – as if she were in limbo up here in this eternal summer – to think sanely about being a great artist. The war was changing everything.

When she told them what she had seen on the news, Uncle Bert said, 'Invasion? Blimey, forget it. The last time this country was ever invaded was ten sixty-six, William the Conqueror.'

But on the wireless the news was very bad. He didn't laugh when he listened, just said, 'Best you're out of London. Your mum ought to come up.'

'Where on earth would we put her?'

Auntie Betty was not terribly good friends with her

sister, Josie knew. They weren't at all alike. Auntie Betty, dumpy and quick like a little robin, with her bright eyes and prattle, was quite different from the austere Edna, Josie's mother. Josie found Auntie Betty much easier to get on with.

'Besides,' Auntie Betty said, 'she's working now. Got a job at Hawker's factory in Kingston.'

'Can't see your sister on the production line,' Bert said.

'I think she's in the office. After all, she worked in an office before she was married. Quite high up, she got. She always had the brains. That's where Josie gets them from.'

'Eh, but you had the looks.'

'Aye, and Josie's got both. She's lucky.'

Josie couldn't believe her mother had taken a job. It made her feel cast-off, her mother leading her own life.

Her aunt and uncle nattered on. Josie never quite knew what to do in the evenings when Bert switched the wireless on. Auntie Betty was always mending or knitting; Maureen read *Woman's Own* and *Woman's Weekly* and knitted a khaki pullover for a soldier; Uncle Bert snored. Josie had always had lots of homework in the past, and now was lost without it. She sketched Uncle Bert and started knitting an air force jumper. The wool was free. Everyone knitted.

'We can find you a job on the farm come harvest,' Uncle Bert said. 'Stooking. It's a busy time.'

'What's stooking?'

Uncle Bert looked at her as if she came from outer space. 'Stooking – why, that's picking up the stooks and laying them upright to dry, four by four. The reaper spits 'em out like, and you follow up behind the horses, and prop 'em up. There's an art to it, mind you, so's they don't slip down, but I daresay you'd pick it up fast enough.'

'Harvest'll be early this year,' Auntie Betty said.

Yawn, yawn, thought Josie. Sometimes she felt herself yearning for the whirr of the trolley-buses down the high street, the crowded shopping counters in Ely's, the smell of tar melting on the pavements. She remembered four of them squashing into the booth in the music shop to try out records under the watchful eye of the disapproving shop assistant, giggling, always giggling. The wonderful roar of Sidney's motorbike down the Kingston bypass, hair flying, cheek pressed hard against Sidney's smelly jacket . . . she was homesick!

Chapter Six

Maureen duly got Josie an evening job at the pub, washing up and making sandwiches on the four nights she wasn't doing it herself. Although the work was not inspiring, the atmosphere was fantastic, as most nights the pilots came down from the airfield to get drunk. They piled six or eight to a broken-down two-seater MG and stayed all night, shouting and singing. How they managed to fly at dawn Josie never could work out. They were mostly very young, patrolling all day over the east coast convoys at sea.

Josie was not allowed in the bar but in lulls in the chores she came out and sat with Jumbo in a corner. Jumbo was accepted into the pilots' circle because they knew, but for his leg, he would have been one of them, and his brother was the ace Chris Patterson whose name was much respected. They didn't mix with any of the other locals. Josie realized that the evenings were balm to Jumbo's tortured soul, being accepted. When he drank too much they drove him home – probably putting him in more danger than if he had staggered along the road on his crutches.

It was a convenient way to carry on their friendship. Being amongst other people took the pressure off. Being together for too long in the lonely, sun-drenched fields and woods around the village gave the affair opportunities neither of them quite wanted to grasp, not yet. Jumbo kissed her tentatively, and she loved the feel of his soft, innocent cheek: he was so sweet after sour Sidney, untouched, his upper-class aura giving her confidence, perhaps unfounded, that he would never upset her, violate her suburban, mother-ridden values: 'Never let a boy touch you, *anywhere*!' The thought made her giggle.

'Why are you laughing?'

'Because I am happy. You are so nice.'

'Do you love me? I think I am beginning to love you.'

'Yes. Perhaps. Beginning.'

'We're not in a hurry, are we? If we're in too much of a hurry, it will be over too soon. Nothing lasts.'

'Crikey, you talk as if you're a hundred and ten!'

'My experiences have aged me.' He grinned at her. Then: 'It hurts too much, to love someone.'

'How can it hurt?'

'In case anything happens. If Chris, for example – it doesn't bear thinking about, and he's only a brother, not a lover.'

Josie realized her experience of love was very limited. Even now, she didn't know what she felt. She loved being with Jumbo, looked forward to being with him every day, parted with regret, yet didn't hanker for the Sidney thing, only the touch of Jumbo's hand, calloused from the crutches. Perhaps there was something wrong with her? She was used to Maureen's panics every time her period was a day late: she went pale, cried into her pillow, went jumping off haystacks . . . it was surely only a matter of time? Josie despised her. She wasn't like that. Nice girls didn't, as far as she knew. The little she knew. None of her friends at school would. Would they? No, all that was for later on. 'To bring shame on the family!' – her mother's words. Whatever would Auntie Betty say if Maureen got pregnant? She had obviously not warned her daughter off fiercely enough. Not like Josie had been warned off.

When they were in the kitchen, Josie doing the ironing and Betty making bread, Betty said, 'That young Jumbo of yours, he's not too forward with you, I hope? All that time you spend alone. I'm supposed to be in charge – you know what your mother's like. But I always trust that he's a gentleman. His upbringing and that, I trust him.'

'Yes, he's all right.'

'It's your mother I'm frightened of. She was a funny one, had a boyfriend who was killed in the last war. She adored him and when he was killed she went almost mad with grief. The only man she had ever looked at. Funny thing, she wasn't really a one for boys and when she did meet Fred – that was his name, Freddie Harbottle – it was a real head-over-heels.

62

Crazy she was for him. We all said steady on, like, because he was at the front, but she always swore he would come home and marry her. Well, she was eighteen when she met him, and twenty when he was killed, the week before the armistice. He'd been home on leave and they were going to be married when Christmas came. But there, he went back and a few days later, that was that. The news came. Poor Edna! We thought she'd never get over it.'

Josie was flabbergasted.

'My mother! I never knew that! She never told me!'

'No, well, I think it's partly why she's such a starchy one now. Between you and me, it killed something in her. She met your father and he was a nice man and she married him but she never had for him what she had for Freddie.'

It made Josie see her mother in a completely different light. Why had she never mentioned any of this to her? Out of loyalty perhaps, to Father? Or was it still too painful to talk about? Josie's head reeled with the story. Had she let Freddie *touch* her, then? Had she lain with him, like that? If she loved him so and he was going back into danger, she must have. Or did she not, and regretted it for ever? Josie longed to know more, but doubted whether she would ever dare bring the subject up with her mother.

'It was a terrible thing to happen,' Auntie Betty said, kneading the bread with her stubby little hands, 'but it was happening all the time. And now it's happening all over again. Will men never learn?'

That night Josie wrote her mother a letter. She always wrote once a week and her mother wrote back. Josie's initial homesickness had worn off, but this time she felt a dreadful ache for her mother. Her mother with her unsympathetic ways, her faded, lined face, her concern for keeping everything right by the neighbours. She did have a heart, a broken heart – what could be more romantic than that? Why had she never spoken of this terrible story? Because it was still too painful? And her patient, silent, unknowable father, did he know that he was only second best, to staunch a wound? It was true what Jumbo had said, that to love someone very much made you a hostage to fortune: some things were out of your hands and you could be terribly hurt. She had never guessed that her mother knew the truth of this so well. And now she felt a strange longing to be at home, putting her arms round her spiky mother and giving her comfort. How to put this in a letter? Impossible.

The harvest was early, as everyone predicted, and Josie went out stooking for half a crown a day. The reaper, pulled by two horses, cut the barley, tied it into bundles and spat them out behind. Josie had to pick up the sheaves in pairs and stub two pairs together in a foursome, heads up, so that they dried out ready for threshing. The barley scratched abominably, the barbs sticking fast in every bit of clothing; the sun was scorching and the work tedious.

The barley field was high up on the crest of a ridge

which overlooked the airfield. For the first time Josie got a view of the Hurricanes actually taking off, one by one, in close formation along the runway. In the hands of the daft, drunken boys from the pub they soared impeccably into the cloudless sky and flew away three by three, in Vs, wingtips almost touching. They came back intermittently in singles, sometimes with holes in, ailerons trailing, a wisp of white vapour following. Occasionally, not at all. In the pub, if one of them had been killed, they drank harder and laughed louder.

'They have to,' Jumbo said. 'How can you go out next day, if you think about it?'

Josie knew he was thinking of Chris, now based in Sussex, in the worst of it. The softening-up process had begun, with bombers attacking shipping in the Channel and in the Thames estuary and starting to drop bombs on towns on the south coast. The fighters had to stop them. But the bombers were escorted by droves of their own fighters, there to keep off the attackers.

'He rings me sometimes. He chooses the times he knows Ma's down the stables and Dad's gone to London. He won't come home. He says he can't face it, he can't leave it. When they have time off they go up to London and live it up, then they go back again. To be alone, he says, lying by a stream somewhere, far away, that would be all right. But not to be with people asking questions, not parents like ours, he said, who show no fear and don't expect anyone else to.'

'But they are afraid for him? *You* are?'

'Yes, of course. And he says he's been sick sometimes, before taking off. And then you fly, and you're fighting, and everything's all right.'

Josie only half understood. She tried to think what it was like, being all happy in the mess, laughing and joking, and then the scramble comes and you know the next minute you might be fighting for your life, or being burned to death in your cockpit, or dangling in the sky from your parachute. Chris had been shot down twice in France, she knew. She had heard dreadful stories of a pilot being burned to death and his radio transmitter still on, broadcasting his terrible screams to his pals as the plane plunged out of the sky.

'But you still want to do it?' she said angrily to Jumbo. 'It's all you talk about, getting back into the RAF.'

'Yes, I do. I do want to do it. I know I'm missing something fantastic, and I should have been in it.'

'And been killed?'

'But you don't think *you* are going to be killed. The *others* get killed. When you're up there, fighting, it's the most exciting thing you'll ever do in your life. It takes you to the limit. I know what Chris feels. He doesn't want to come away from it. It's why he won't come home.'

Josie wasn't at all sure about Jumbo's attitude. He felt like this because he was frustrated in his dreams. But Chris knew he couldn't get out of it even if he wanted to, so had to make a philosophy to see him through. She couldn't imagine what the truth of it was.

But one morning, when she was out in the fields stooking, she witnessed her first dogfight at close hand. Not just the whorls of vapour trails so high up that you couldn't distinguish the planes at all, but a vicious fight between two Hurricanes and two Messerschmitt 109s that was clearly in focus from start to finish.

It started with a distant chatter of machine-gun fire which made them all straighten up with a jerk. Uncle Bert stopped the reaper and Josie stood clasping her two sheaves of corn to her bosom, squinting up into the sun where the noise came from. Everything then happened so fast it was hard to take in, the planes spinning down out of the sky, zooming desperately up again, rolling and falling out of spins like tossed pennies, all the time with vicious bursts of fire-power punctuating their antics. For a few minutes they zoomed away and disappeared completely, then suddenly one of the Hurricanes came back with a Messerschmitt on its tail, firing. Behind it was the other Hurricane, also firing.

Josie supposed afterwards that she should have flung herself to the ground like people did in the cinema but, hypnotized by the action, she just stood gaping. The leading Hurricane shuddered and Josie could actually see bits flying off it. A white stream erupted from somewhere up front and it banked, perilously close to the ground, making for the airfield, streaming white vapour. The Messerschmitt pulled violently out of its dive and twisted up, rocking victoriously, but fire from the Hurricane following must have made a mark; for it flattened out abruptly and seemed to stagger. The Hurricane screamed past and flung round in an impossible turn to attack again, overshot in its excitement, and zoomed momentarily out of sight. The Messerschmitt, clearly in trouble, coughed irresolutely and started to lose height, skimming towards the far ridge of trees. The Hurricane then returned and poured another burst of fire into it, at which the Messerschmitt blew up and crashed spectacularly into the copse. A pillar of fire exploded into the sky. The Hurricane flew over it in a wide circle and then came back over the field where Josie was working, waggling its wings in triumph. Josie had a glimpse of the young pilot's face, ecstatic, goggles pushed up into wild, baby-blond hair, while she was still trying to take in the fact of death where the great black plume of smoke was hanging over the woods. The men were cheering and shouting, but she felt sick. It had all happened so fast, and was so violent, that she felt almost as if she had taken part. She found she was shaking all over, still clutching her golden sheaves, like an advertisement for bread.

Uncle Bert came over to her.

'Are you all right, gel? That were smashing, eh? Give 'em a bit of what for, the blooming Nazis, eh?'

He said it like Churchill: Narzies. But Josie thought:

He wasn't a Narzi; he was just a young boy like the one who had killed him, triumphant.

'Yes, it was smashing!'

Better him than one of theirs. She had to convince herself.

The village was agog with the excitement. The pub that evening toasted the young blond boy, who was getting disastrously drunk. It was his first bag. He gave Josie a kiss when she was standing there with Jumbo. But all Josie could think of was the other pilot, as young and as brave, who had been blown out of the sky. He had a mother too, and maybe a girl who loved him.

If Auntie Betty hadn't told her the story about her mother, perhaps she wouldn't have given him a thought, but just joined in the rejoicing. Uncle Bert was full of it. But Auntie Betty shook her head and said she was glad she hadn't been watching.

'I was mangling in the kitchen. I got in the cupboard under the stairs when I heard the gunfire. I thought it might be bombs. Maybe you should dig an air-raid shelter, Bert, like them in London.'

'I do enough digging,' Bert said. 'Leave it out.'

'Being so near the airfield's no joke. What if they come bombing them like they promised? Josie's safer in Wimbledon.'

'Look, if our number's on it, that's it, whether we're in London, here or Timbuctoo. What's the use of worrying?'

'Better not write your mother about it, Josie, else she'll be worrying too.'

'I don't want to go home.'

It was true: in spite of her occasional pangs of home-sickness and twists of longing to see her parents again, she preferred life here in the country. Now that she had the fun of the evenings in the pub, Jumbo's lively company and their jolly outings to the cinema and fish and chips, life seemed very pleasant. Even the stook-ing was nearly over, early, in the first week of August.

But in the skies the fighters were busier by the day. The boys in the pub lost four more pilots and the squadron was posted away to South Wales to protect Bristol, a quieter life than over the Thames estuary. Another squadron would soon be drafted in. In the meantime it was strangely quiet and peaceful. It was hard to believe there was a war on.

Chapter Seven

Jumbo said, 'My mother has invited you to lunch. It's a summons.'

'Golly! What for?'

'She wants to examine you, to see if you're fit to be my girlfriend.'

'Oh, Jumbo, no!'

'Oh, sorry, I'm not being very tactful, am I? She wants to meet you, that's all. Quite harmless. Macaroni cheese. My pa won't be there, just the three of us.'

Jumbo grinned. His suntanned face was coming out in freckles and his hair was bleached by the sun. He was so open, so optimistic, such good company, Josie had to laugh. She flung her arms round him.

'I would do anything for you!'

'Even meet my mother?'

'Yes, yes.'

'You're a winner, Josie! What would I do without you?'

'And me? How lucky we met!'

Josie knew she was falling in love. How could she

not? He was so lovely, so kind, so funny. It was true: for Jumbo now she would do anything, even meet his mother.

'Oh, she's a tartar, that one,' said Auntie Betty. 'I don't know how she produced such nice boys. You mind your ps and qs, gel.'

It was no good pretending that she was not nervous. Although she had been up to Nightingales a few times with Jumbo, she had never met his mother, because she spent all her time in the stables, which were down a drive at the back of the house. Josie didn't like being at Nightingales because of Maureen being around. It embarrassed her to come to the house as a guest when Maureen was there being the maid. Luckily the day she was invited wasn't a Maureen day. Maureen said Jumbo was a saint.

'You're so lucky, having him,' she sighed to Josie in their bedroom. 'You can trust someone like that. He's so – so sweet. He doesn't treat me like she does. She treats me like dirt. He's just normal, like you're one of them.'

Josie knew that Maureen was having trouble with Tom. She had colossal rows with him, mainly because she had a very jealous nature. She had seen him talking to another girl, and Maureen did not allow that. Josie tried to reason with her, but to no avail. Josie privately thought Tom would be far better off with someone else. He was quite a nice, dim, laughing boy, not looking for trouble, only sex.

Maureen said of Jumbo, 'I don't know how he bears

it, waiting for his leg. Sometimes he just sits in his room, staring out of the window, or lying on his bed, staring at the ceiling. I clean the room and he doesn't move, doesn't say anything. Sometimes I almost think he's been crying. It must be awful for him when everything's happening out there.'

This shook Josie. She had never seen this side of Jumbo.

'He said September, for his leg. They told him,' she said.

'Not long now then.' And then, with a sigh, 'You *are* lucky.'

Josie supposed that she must be in love because she was so happy all the time. Every morning she woke up it seemed like another day in paradise. Every day was better than the one before. She tried not to listen to the news, which was terrible; it was something she kept in another compartment. The more they were hurrying to their doom, the happier her life became. It could only be love. And at least one-legged Jumbo was safe; she did not have to fear for his life, like so many poor girls. It was hard to imagine how terrible that must be.

He came to meet her on the day of the lunch, hopping down the drive.

'She's not changed out of her joddies for you, so she's not expecting much,' he said cheerfully.

'I've dressed up for her! Or haven't you noticed?' Her favourite dress, a linen thing printed with faded flowers in green and orange. Mostly she wore grey flannel shorts and an aertex shirt. 'I put a dress on.'

'So you did. And me a clean shirt.'

They giggled and Jumbo propped his crutches up against a laurel bush so that he could take her in his arms and kiss her. He rubbed his nose into her dark curls and said, 'You've made my life worth living these last few weeks.' He kissed her ear and her cheek and her lips. 'You do smell nice.'

'You smell of Wright's Coal Tar.'

'That's all we get in our bathroom.'

'Mine's Muguet des Bois. Yardley. I think it means lily of the valley.'

'My little lily.'

He kissed her more ardently and his face flushed. 'I do love you. I'm beginning to love you an awful lot.'

'Yes.'

'What do you mean, yes?' He stopped her reply with another passionate kiss and she put her arms round his neck and pushed her fingers into his hair, holding him closer. He lost his balance and fell over and Josie fell over in his arms, so they lay on the gravel drive laughing and kissing.

'God, the postman's due. It'll be all round the village. Get up, you hussy.'

Jumbo pushed her away. 'Attacking a disabled man like that, you ought to be ashamed of yourself!'

'My shoes are full of gravel.'

Josie hopped about, emptying them, Jumbo retrieved his crutches and they giggled their way up to the front door. Jumbo swung up the steps. The door

74

was open and several spaniels came rushing out, bobbed tails spinning.

'Ma's back then. Come into the lion's den.'

The house showed few signs of gracious living, although the unpolished furniture was antique and valuable, if it had been cared for. Huge oil paintings of hunting scenes and dog portraits scattered the high walls, and tarnished silver cups and trophies were arranged higgledy-piggledy on most flat surfaces. A wide curving staircase with a threadbare carpet rose up from the end of the hall, intimations of grandeur unfulfilled. Mrs Patterson was no homemaker. (Maureen had said her job consisted mostly of cleaning up the dog hair; there was no time for polishing).

Jumbo led Josie into the kitchen, where his mother was putting something into the oven. Josie took in this tall, spare, hard-featured woman. Jumbo, like herself, hadn't got a cuddly mother. Where had they missed out?

'Josie, how nice to meet you.' She advanced for a firm handshake. She smiled. Her eyes missed nothing. Josie was glad she was in her best frock, and hoped no leaves or mud were stuck on her back.

'Good morning,' she said stupidly.

'The lunch will be ten minutes. Would you like a sherry while we wait? Jumbo dear, see to it, will you?'

A sherry, blimey! Josie had never drunk sherry in her life. Nor anything else come to that, save the pub's ginger beer.

'Thank you, yes.'

She sat down at the kitchen table as Mrs Patterson pulled a chair out for her and Jumbo came hopping in with a bottle of sherry.

'Sorry, can't do the silver tray and glasses. Beyond me capabilities.'

'Don't be silly. The glasses are in here, as you well know.'

Breath of cold air. Blimey, thought Josie again, out of her depth. Jumbo brought the glasses from the dresser. They were cut glass and probably worth ten pounds each: Josie was remembering Maureen's washing-up story.

Then suddenly, with the sherry poured, the woman's hard face turned sort of glittery: a great smile swooped across the taut cheeks and she turned to Jumbo and said, 'Darling, what do you think? Chris rang up an hour ago and said he's been posted here, to our own airfield. His squadron's coming up from Kent. Sheer fluke, he said. Amazing, isn't it?'

Jumbo, like his mother, was transformed with joy. His face lit up and he laughed out loud. 'My God, that's wizard! Chris! Oh, it's incredible! What a piece of luck, landing up here! Oh, Ma, how wonderful!'

Josie was equally astonished by this turn of events, particularly by the effect it had on mother and son. Like God coming.

'He said they'd be operational from dawn to dusk, not to get excited about his coming to lunch or any-thing, but all the same . . . to know he's just down the road – that's quite something after all this time. We haven't seen him since that weekend he came home from France. Let's drink to it, shall we?'

She held up her sherry glass and clinked it with Jumbo's and Josie had to clink hers too. It was like in the pub with the beer tankards: 'Here's to the old sod! Bottoms up!' Generally when the old sod had failed to come back from a sortie.

'So, it's a celebration, Josie, you've chosen the right day! Aren't we lucky!'

It was apparent that the news had transformed both of them. Mrs Patterson was charming, not at all as Josie had been expecting, and Jumbo was as excited as if the date for his new leg had come. There was this sudden bond between them that Josie thought was probably rare.

When they had finished the macaroni cheese, the haggard look came back into Mrs Patterson's face and she said bitterly: 'This war! Having Chris so close, knowing what he's doing every day . . . I try not to think about it. After what your father has suffered all his life, what is the point of it all?'

'He was blinded by friendly fire, can you believe?' Jumbo said to Josie. 'He walked into an occupied building and they thought he was a jerry and a bloke shot him in the face. And he never complained. The soldier who shot him went to see him in hospital, and after the war they met up and became the best of friends.'

'Golly!' Josie's head whirled. 'How could they do that?'

'Oh yes, I can see how they could. After all, for the man who blinded him, it must have been just as terrible in its own way. And Dad was a lieutenant colonel, no less, and the man just a private. Imagine! Of course Dad took the blame, said it was his own fault. It wasn't really, I don't think. But it doesn't do to blame other people for what happens to you when it's in all innocence.'

He spoke very sombrely, as if with some personal feeling. Josie felt unable to take part in this conversation: it was completely out of her experience.

'One must live for the day,' said Mrs Patterson. 'It helps to be optimistic. Your father might have nursed bitterness all his life, but he just got on with it. It's the only way. Courage.'

She then smiled happily at Josie and said, 'Do you ride, dear? Where you come from – the riding's very good on Wimbledon Common.'

'No, I've never.' She didn't like to say it was too expensive for the likes of her parents. Not that she had ever wanted to.

'I have a friend, Reggie, who keeps a horse in Wimbledon, and there's Jean with her yard by the common, and Phyllis and Joy. I used to ride in Richmond Park once – very beautiful. You get to know people in the horse world, meet them all over. It's great fun, you know.'

'Yes,' murmured Josie. The thought of riding a horse appalled her.

'It's nice Jumbo's found a friend to while away the

hours. Don't let him lead you astray, my dear. He was very wild before. The two of them were, very wild.'

'We're tame now,' Jumbo said. 'Tame as two kittens. Don't worry.'

'Tamed by events, I'm afraid. Do you want a pudding? We've got strawberries, I think, if Percy picked them.'

She looked vaguely around the kitchen and found a bowl of strawberries underneath some newspapers. She brought them to the table and they ate them out of the bowl. They were slightly muddy but delicious.

'Thank God Percy's too old to join the army. I couldn't do without him. And Tilly. It's Tilly's day off today.'

'What does Tilly do on her day off?' Jumbo asked.

'She gets up late, goes down to the village for a gossip, works on her rug for a bit, then she gets bored and comes down here to see if there's anything that needs doing.'

Jumbo laughed.

They cleared the plates and Josie offered to wash up but Mrs Patterson laughed and said, 'Gracious, no! Tilly will do it later.'

She went back to her stables and Jumbo said, 'That wasn't so bad, was it?'

'No. I was dreading it and she was really nice.'

'Smashing news about Chris. That's what's made her so happy, to see him again. He's her favourite boy. And mine too.'

Josie was curious to meet this paragon. The village

was very quiet now that the squadron had moved, and everyone was awaiting the arrival of the new battle-hardened crack squadron, geared up to take their part in what Churchill was calling the battle of Britain, no less.

Chapter Eight

'I don't know that you're any safer here than at home now,' Auntie Betty said anxiously to Josie. She was hanging out the washing and an ailing Hurricane had narrowly missed the garden before making a crash-landing on the edge of the airfield. Josie had run out to look.

'They say the Germans are going to bomb the airfields to try and stop the fighters. It says in the papers.'

'Well, Mum said in her last letter that they had had bombs just down the road, so what's the difference?'

'I'll write to her and see what she says. Pity we're none of us on the phone.'

Now, with Jumbo, Josie desperately didn't want to go home. Even her ambitions to go to art school were on hold. Life was delicious, war or no war.

The new squadron had been virtually in the sky ever since it had arrived three days ago. The pilots hadn't yet appeared in the pub and Chris had not yet surfaced. It was mid August and the cloudless southern skies were scored with the fighters' vapour trails, often so high that one could only hear the faintest whine of engines; occasionally, as now, scorchingly low, with sometimes the clatter of machine-gun fire as one fighter chased another, hedge-hopping in desperation. German bombers in vast fleets were attacking, or trying to attack, Portsmouth and Southampton, the Kentish ports and aerodromes and the ships in the Thames estuary. They were accompanied by hordes of fighters trying to protect them. The fighting was fierce and the casualties on both sides high. Josie had seen a bomber come down over the ridge of trees beyond the manor, and three parachutes blossoming like flowers in the sky – thank goodness too far away for her to run and interfere. The farmers were full of talk about rounding up the Jerries, shotguns to hand.

Jumbo went to London with his father to see about fixing digs with a family friend in Richmond for when he got his new leg. He would have to stay around the prosthetics hospital for a few weeks for fittings and practice. Josie took the opportunity to go back to the manor and do some drawing.

She had grown to love this spot, which she felt was her own. Apart from Jumbo, she had never met anyone else here. It was quite deserted, and enchanted in its summer somnolence, with just the white swans drifting on the lake and the moorhens chuck-chucking in the reeds. One could not believe that death and disaster were all around, so tranquil was the setting. Sometimes she just wanted to sit and take it in, absorb the peace, knowing that it was as fragile as the wings of the dragonflies that hovered over the water. It was impossible to think of the coming invasion, the cruelty of war, lying in the sweet-scented grass under the canopy of bright leaves where the birds sang and busied about their nests. Sometimes it made her cry, just thinking about it. She could feel her emotions stretching common-sense, so that sometimes she felt she was on the edge of reason, longing for something impossible even to know. Was this all about being in love? Or her age, as her mother used to darkly imply when she was unreasonable at home? And she remembered Mrs Patterson with her public-school sang-froid: don't make a fuss, get on with it, don't give way to silly emotion. What would she do if Chris were killed? Josie wondered. Lift her chin higher, no doubt. But in the solitude of the manor's grounds, Josie felt no compunction in occasionally giving way, letting tears run down her cheeks as she thought of her own happiness, the unknowable future, the impossibility of even understanding herself. She had a feeling sometimes that she was completely alone in the world, even though there was Jumbo. She knew she missed the companionship of her school days severely, having no equally disorientated girlfriends to discuss her problems with.

But what problems? she thought now, sitting with her back to a big beech tree in her favourite spot overlooking the lake. Jumbo was away but he would be back in a couple of days. She was about to paint her favourite view, enjoying the exercise of improving on the result all the time. It gave enormous satisfaction to get it right, so that afterwards one kept going back to look at the drawing, congratulating oneself, until the pleasure got stale and it was time to start another. If one had no distractions, like being in love, she could see that being an artist was all-consuming.

She laid out her paints. She was not on the edge of the wood, but back inside it so that she had some trees in front of her, and the focus of the painting would be the view between, of the swans on the lake. The swans would be very small, pinpricks of white in the sun on the water, with all the frame round being the shade under the trees. It could be stunning if she were clever enough to make it work. But how well she knew the abyss between what she saw in her head and what arrived on the paper! It was pretty difficult, after all. She wasn't Gainsborough. Yet. But her optimism soared, so that instead of her stupid crying she was suddenly bursting with happiness about her brilliant future and dear Jumbo. She had all afternoon ahead of her, without interruption.

It was very hot, without a breeze. The summer had been unusually brilliant, as if nature wanted to contradict what stupid humans were up to. Far away came the familiar sound of a returning fighter, for which Josie now rarely bothered to look up. This one was damaged – she could tell by the stuttering of the engine – but she guessed it would make the airfield: it was near enough.

But then she stopped drawing. The sound was much too near for comfort.

'Crikey!'

She knocked her jar of water over in horror as the aeroplane came into sight, heading straight towards her, just brushing the far trees as it dropped down over the lake. She could see shot-up ailerons trailing from its wings and the tail half-destroyed with a great hole through the rudder. Although it was obviously going to land, or try to, there were no wheels down. The wings rocked and the plane seemed to hover over the lake like a monstrous predator. Then, by what Josie felt was an enormous effort, its nose turned for the great sweep of the erstwhile lawn and instead of plunging into the water it hit the grass on the edge of the lake and went careering up towards the house, tearing great clods out with its belly, its propeller crumpling, lumps of aeroplane flying off in all directions. It made a terrible racket but, in the space of seconds – the time for the whole incident to have taken place – there was the ineffable silence again. From far away, the whirring of a woodpecker. No more, no less.

Josie was standing up, shocked rigid.

She knew the aeroplane might blow up at any minute, but it didn't. It lay like a beached whale, smoking and shuddering. The cockpit canopy was already open. In a few seconds a figure struggled out, with great difficulty, and slithered down onto the wing, then dropped to the ground.

Josie, for reasons she never understood, shouted, 'Over here! Come over here!'

Her voice carried shrilly, and the pilot started to stumble towards the sound of her voice. She doubted if he could see her for his face was covered with blood.

'Here, over here!'

She realized she was trembling like a leaf. What did she have to staunch blood with? Her paint-rag, half of one of Auntie Betty's retired tea-towels, a small handkerchief . . .

'What the hell . . .?'

The pilot came through the trees, pulling off his helmet and oxygen mask, holding his hand up to his face. Dark hair tumbled over his oil-streaked forehead.

'What—?'

He took in the spread rug, the thermos of tea and packet of sandwiches in the basket she always took with her on painting expeditions – the gentle perquisites of an English summer picnic – and he just smiled and said, 'Paradise,' fell onto the rug and passed out.

Josie's heart was thudding like a steam-engine. She stood staring at the prostrate figure, trying to get her wits together. She had time now. The blood was coming from his nose, not so terrible; he seemed all in one piece otherwise. She thought he must have knocked his head in the violent landing. There was oil all over him and all round his face except where the oxygen mask had been. His smile in unconsciousness was very beautiful. He was extraordinarily handsome, very young, but with a gauntness about the cheek-bones, and already lines of care around the eyes.

She knelt down beside him. She wondered if she ought to go for help. He might be badly injured in places she couldn't see. But his breathing was easy and his colour only a little pale, not blueish: he didn't groan or sigh, but muttered once, 'You bastard!' and twitched like a dreaming dog. Josie wiped the blood away with the half tea-towel, very gently, and was relieved to see there was no more. After a bit she sat down beside him. She could not leave him, she felt, even to get help. She just sat there, waiting.

The smoke from the Hurricane died down. It lay like a wounded dinosaur on the scored grass, a strange aberration in Josie's serene landscape. The silence returned, save for the whirring woodpecker. Josie waited.

After a little while she heard the noise of a motor coming from the drive behind the house. The engine stopped and in a few moments some men came running round the ruins. They saw the plane and stopped dead. There were four of them, in air force uniform. They had a short conversation, then approached the plane. Josie could see quite plainly that they were dreading what they might find in the cockpit: she could feel their dread from where she sat, see it in the forced footfalls. The first man reached the plane and peered in.

'Empty!'

His voice rang in relief and triumph, and immediately the figures broke into laughter and animation. A distance away, Josie felt she was watching a performance on stage. She could not hear all their words but she could tell from their attitudes as they examined the plane that they were full of amazement and awe that anyone could have survived the wreck of the machine. She could hear 'Bloody hell!' and 'You going to mend this one, Staffy?' Laughter. And then 'Where's the blighter got to then?' 'Probably walking back.'

Josie got up, hesitant.

But the pilot lying on the rug rolled over and said, 'Don't move. Stay still.'

'They can help you, take you back. They've got a car.'

'I want to stay here with you. Lie doggo. Sit down.'

They came looking, smashing through the trees, shouting, 'Chris! Chris, where are you?'

Josie knew it was Chris.

'You're Jumbo's brother?'

'Yes.'

She could see that, even if he wasn't injured, he was totally exhausted, whether from what had just happened or long-term exhausted she couldn't tell.

The searchers came dangerously close, threshing through the trees.

Then one of them said, 'He'll have gone back to the road, surely? It's a waste of time messing about here. If we don't find him back at base we can come back with a proper search party.'

'He knows his way around here. It's his home.'

'Yeah. Could have gone up to the farm. We'll try there.'

They went away and disappeared round the side of the house. All was quiet again. Chris rolled round and propped himself on one elbow. He looked at Josie.

'How about the picnic then? I'm starving.'

Josie was startled. 'But shouldn't you tell them – go back?'

'Why? They might give me the rest of the day off if I'm lucky, and I'd rather spend it here than in the mess. And if I fall asleep, which I will, I would rather sleep here than in my bed. You don't mind?'

'No, of course not! But – but – you're all right? Not hurt?'

'I hit my head when we pranged, that's all. No. But I got that bastard, the same time as he did for me. I saw him crash into the estuary. I thought I'd get home but at the last minute the steering went – so here we are. I thought I was a goner coming over the lake. I thought what a bloody silly place to die, the very place I spent all my childhood, fishing in that lake and making rafts with Jumbo!'

He sat up, frowning, and started to shrug out of his leather flying jacket. Josie saw the purple and white stripes of his DFC badge on his uniform as he pulled off a scarf and unbuttoned his jacket. It was very hot; beads of perspiration stood out on his forehead. Josie unscrewed the thermos and poured the tea into the bakelite beaker.

'Here.'

He drank the whole of the thermos and wolfed the limp sandwiches. Josie thought his need far greater than hers and he made no apology.

'I would like this to last for ever,' he said. 'To come down like that, and then find you with your picnic, looking like a fairy from the lake, to pour me tea. Jumbo always said there were fairies in the lake. I told him not to be so stupid. Bogeys more like, I said, monsters. But there, he was right.'

He smiled. Josie could see already why girls, as Jumbo said, fell out of the trees for him. He spoke this rubbish quite seriously, sincerely, and Josie realized exactly what it meant to someone who less than half an hour ago had killed a man and then come within an ace of losing his own life, to then find himself at peace in this idyllic glade. To handle the situation as he did, without histrionics, was no doubt the outcome of his spartan upbringing, the fearsome mothering. But apparently calm as he was, Josie saw that his hands were trembling: the tea shook, and there was an aura of intense strain about him. Josie wanted terribly to mother him.

'You must rest here. Go to sleep. I will look after you. If anyone comes, I will see that it is all right.'

And he lay down again and was asleep in an instant.

He slept all day and woke only as the sun was going down, and only then because Josie shook him awake.

She knew the dew would fall and he needed proper food and care. She knew also that Auntie Betty would be worried sick about her not coming back, but she wouldn't leave him there alone. She felt he needed her. He needed looking after. He moaned and twitched in his sleep and once shouted out the word 'Peter!' as if in warning, which made Josie jump.

It was the strangest day she had ever spent. She did not feel impatient or bored, just sitting there. She felt that what she was doing was very important, not just for Chris but for herself. She had never experienced such a close acquaintance with death: it took a while to sink in. The contrast of the emotions experienced within the tranquillity of the surroundings made it so weird, surreal. She had thought the aeroplane was going to kill her; then that it would kill him, blow up before he got out. But it lay now, somnolent as its pilot, small tatters of its torn fabric fluttering in the soft breeze, and its pilot lay peacefully in the aftermath of horror with the patterns of light and shade from the leaves above blending his body to the ground, and it was as if nothing had happened at all.

So this was the adored Chris, whom she had heard so much about, the one all Jumbo's girlfriends ditched him for! If looks came into it she could see why, with his perfectly honed features and gaunt cheekbones, the tumble of dark hair over the high, bloody forehead. He wasn't yet twenty, but looked ten years older. It was strange being able to stare at him as long as she liked. She wasn't sure what colour his eyes were.

Jumbo's were greenish, but she thought Chris's were blue. His ears were very nice. He had his mother's stern jaw. If the Gestapo caught him he would not blab under torture, she decided. He had already been captured once, according to Jumbo, but had escaped. She sat looking, making up stories. He out-biggled Biggles, she decided, and he was in her possession, asleep on her rug. It was magical.

The last of the Hurricanes came back as the afternoon sank into a golden evening, and Chris stirred, and she put her hand on his shoulder.

'I think we should go now.'

He opened his eyes. Yes, they were blue, dark like his mother's.

Josie thought she was falling in love. Not happily, compliantly, as with Jumbo. But in a seriously uncontrolled, dangerous and totally hopeless way, with his brother. Like a Hurricane crashing.

Chris let the child walk him back. She was like something out of a dream, an elf from the lake with her tender eyes and soft, golden, freckle-spotted skin. He knew he was slightly concussed but he let the dream take him. He had had his fill of the peroxide blondes who chased him with shrieks of joy, to catch 'a hero' with a gong, eight jerries in his bag. He had drunk and danced and lain with them to cover up the pain of living, obliterate the fear, to blank out what would happen tomorrow. Nothing was real. But she was out of a fairytale, leading him out of the fairy forest, out across the golden stubble to the road to the aerodrome. He could see his own home on the further hillside, but had no desire to go there. He would rather go home with his fairy.

'Where do you live?'

She told him.

'They will be worried about me. I have to go back. But I will find you someone with a car, if you want, call on your parents perhaps, and tell them what has happened. What's best?'

'No, I'll walk back to the base. Not my parents. I feel fine to walk – time to think. I have to fill out a report, try and remember what happened. That sleep's set me up. It's not just me, we all fall asleep the minute we sit down. Sorry about that. We start at dawn, pretty early, you see.'

'Won't you have a day off, after that?'

'Well, no. I'm in one piece. I'll probably get a bollocking for not getting back sooner.'

'I think you might be concussed a bit. You ought to have a rest.'

'It'll look as if I'm skiving. I can't say that. Got to show a few bullet holes and blood to get a day off.'

They parted when they got to the road.

Chris said, 'I hope I see you again.'

'I work in the pub at nights. You might see me there, with Jumbo.'

'Are you Jumbo's girlfriend?'

'Yes.'

'I thought you might be. You're Josie?'

'Yes.'

'Goodbye, Josie.'

'Goodbye.'

'For now.'

Josie walked home along the road. She thought she had fallen in love. Love at first sight. But she was Jumbo's girlfriend. How would that work out? It wouldn't.

She walked in a dream, in the silence of the dusk, with the faintest of faint stars beginning to sprinkle the sky. She felt she was balancing on a stretched thread over unknowable depths, at her limit, in other hands than her own. She felt slightly mad, unhinged. Of course she hadn't eaten a thing all day and perhaps was a bit faint, and perhaps shocked by the horror of the plane screaming towards her over the lake, but she did feel very strange.

Auntie Betty and Uncle Bert were, as she expected, worried to death and embraced her with great exclamations of relief.

'We were even thinking of going down to Constable Hawkins, we were that worried! And then I said maybe you were up at the big house, seeing as you had lunch there the other day, but then I remembered Jumbo's gone to London. Oh dear, I have been in a tizzy!'

Josie told them what had happened.

'I couldn't leave him.'

'There, I said to Bert there's a plane come down by

the old manor, but he said you'd gone painting up beyond the airfield, in Fox's Spinney.'

Josie remembered that she had said that, and had changed her mind. Thank goodness they hadn't come looking!

'And it was Jumbo's brother? Just fancy that! He might have been killed under your very eyes!'

Auntie Betty bustled around the kitchen, making Josie a plate of scrambled eggs, chatting away. Uncle Bert sat puffing at his pipe in his armchair, listening to the wireless.

Josie slowly came back to earth. But somehow it wasn't the same earth any more.

Chapter Nine

Strange how, once you were in the cockpit and moving across the ground, the sick dread of the waiting period gave way to confidence and a surge of anticipation, even excitement. It happened every time. Grim, hideous awakening to the pearly dawn light, the longing, *longing*, to go on sleeping, the jitters coming to bug you, the awful, fleeting memories of dead friends, burning aircraft, ripped parachutes hurtling to ground . . . all obliterated in the sudden thrust of power as the throttle was opened and the nose pointed down the runway. Chris's eyes were on the plane of his close friend and leader, Peter Palmer, to keep on his wingtip. Chris was the squadron leader's number two, utterly trusted. They had survived France together, would survive the present onslaught, God willing.

The sun was coming up in a great explosion of red fire over the somnolent countryside. A field of sheep was a spotted square, white dots on green, amongst the waves of striped stubble, long shadows cast before strips of woodland. It reminded Chris of picture books of his childhood, of farm settings where the only quarrels were between geese, or pigs, and the good farmer sorted them, and the little children laughed and played. The sky was an empty canopy, a heavenly playground for a man in a plane who could soar and dip and dive like a bird, its beauty in the sunrise heart-rending. Strange to feel these sweet emotions when on the way to do battle. If one could divorce the purpose of the flight from the moment, his heart would be soaring along with his gallant plane. In fact, it was possible. He would not have changed places with anyone as he flew wingtip to wingtip with his companions, all of whom, he knew, harboured exactly the same mixed feelings. Every day they were torn with exultation, fear, shock, ecstasy, by the nature of the game, or steeped in the boredom of waiting, the sick-ness of anticipation, the fear of showing fear. The relief in the evening, when dark stopped operations and drink blotted out the unbearable strain of the way they were living, was the balm that rounded off their days.

And today, momentarily, the elfin face of the girl by the lake kept appearing in his vision, with little shocks of sweet surprise. It must be the concussion. He had told base he had passed out in the wood, no mention of the picnic, the solace, the magic of that girl's presence. They had not queried it; he had passed a quick medical and been given a brand-new plane, no repercussions. Shipping in the Thames estuary was being attacked; he was now off to shoot down the attackers. This sweet preliminary would soon be ended.

The call came.

'Red leader, a hundred plus approaching Harwich at angels twelve. Many bandits. Keep a good look-out. Over.'

'OK. Understood. Climbing hard through angels seven. On course. Over.'

Throttle wide open to climb, eyes wide open to catch first sight of the invaders . . . difficult, the sun in their eyes when they looked eastward where the sea lay glinting and burnished. But the visibility was boundless. Like a cloud of gnats the bombers were coming in, and above them an umbrella of Messerschmitt 109s. Twelve Hurricanes against God knew how many Jerries. Was it ever any different? Break them up if you were lucky, pray another squadron was on its way.

'Tally-ho, lads. Here we go! Take your pick!' Peter's voice was excited, fired up.

Chris broke away from Peter, heading for the nearest Dornier. Get in fast and give it a blast, hoping he hasn't seen you . . . with luck hurt him and, when the fighters pounce, use every trick in the book to avoid them.

Amazingly they took the bombers by surprise. Chris took his nose on, firing straight into it and ducking underneath at the last moment, a risky manoeuvre, so close that the bomber blowing up could have blown him up too. He soared up and over on his back as a German fighter screamed down on him. The

Messerschmitt's tracer streamed past his cockpit hood. His lovely brand-new plane! He threw it over and went into a spin and the Messerschmitt came after him, turning tightly to get him in his sights. Chris knew the German plane had the edge on his Hurricane, but guessed that his flying skills had the edge on the German pilots. His charmed life – so far – was more due to expertise than luck, he knew that. And so it proved, as the German pilot in his excitement seemed not to realize how close the ground was getting. When Chris pulled out he could read the number plate of a car on the road below (the driver, panicking, had driven into a ditch), and when the German pulled out he hit some telegraph wires, which Chris had flown under, and immediately cartwheeled into a hedgerow and burst into flames.

Chris roared up, exultant. His little plane zoomed up into the brilliant sky, triumphant. Chris knew from experience that this was when another fighter could catch you unawares, unseen, but he twisted and turned, straining to see into the sun, the danger area. He still had plenty of fuel and ammo, which was more than most of the Jerries could boast. They were mostly at the farthest point their fuel could carry them if they wanted enough to return safely: Chris knew only too well from experience the feeling of crossing the Channel with the fuel gauge nearly on zero – more frightening by far than engaging in battle, the terrible loneliness of the water below, even on a sunny day, petrifying the gut. More pilots died in the sea than in fighting. What good was a parachute jump into the Channel? Only a matter of prolonging the agony. Better to hit it in the plane and be killed in the force of the crash. They did not float, their little machines, but took their pilots far, far below onto the seabed, a deep and lonely grave in the bosom of the planet.

The bombers were broken up now and most of them heading back out to sea. A Hurricane plumed down towards the fields, trailing white smoke. Too far away to make out who it was. Its dive steepened to the vertical but no one jumped out. Chris spun away, climbing, climbing, not wanting to know, angry now, his mood switched. The *bastards*! What were they doing here, over this sweet countryside, far from home? The sky was full of white vapour trails, the crazy patterns of battle swirling white against the blue.

Suddenly, there was Peter in deep trouble with three Messerschmitts on his tail. Zipping out of range of one he came into the burst from the second. Chris saw bits of aeroplane flying off his fuselage and the third begger lining up astern to finish him off. None of them saw Chris. Surprise was his advantage as he dived in with a long, optimistic burst at the astern attacker, erratic but enough to make the German pilot dive away in panic. Peter jinked out of trouble. Chris crossed underneath him and found the pale blue belly of a Messerschmitt filling his sights. He pressed the button: too late, the plane was gone, but glycol from a punctured radiator made a pleasant white plume behind him.

'Get home if you can, you beggar!'

The enemy planes were now out of ammo and worried about fuel and set sail for home. Chris and Peter went for some departing shots to help them on their way, then waggled their wings at each other and turned for home. Enough was enough. The sky was suddenly empty, the pulses calmed. Chris was drenched in sweat. He pulled off mask and helmet and felt the glorious morning swoop across his burning face. He was still alive, thank God! The adrenalin surged and he did a few forbidden acrobatics, skimming home across the fields. Peter was there still, holes torn in his tail, fabric fluttering wildly, but grinning like a maniac. A few hours respite, breakfast if they were lucky, then up again at the telephone's command, usually at least three times a day. What a life! No wonder they were getting wrinkles, old before their time. They screamed in their sleep, their hands trembled, they had no conviction that they would still be alive in twelve hours' time. But it could not be otherwise: they depended utterly on each other; the bond between them was invincible. It barred outsiders; its camaraderie was absolute, they would not have had it otherwise. Living life when so close to death made it more glorious. Chris had experienced something of the same dichotomy in the mountains, taking a risk too far, a handspan from disaster. If he came through this, which he knew in his heart that he wouldn't, the life to come was an unimaginable void.

When they landed, trundling in to be greeted with

relief and excitement by their faithful ground crew, unstrapped, helped out, relieved of parachute and life jacket, Chris walked with Peter back to the debriefing. No talk of who wasn't home, who was in the Hurricane that dived into the ground, only anticipation of the reports they had to make out: one Messerschmitt for sure, on Chris's part, but only a probable for the Dornier, as he hadn't seen it hit the ground; one Messerschmitt for Peter. A worthwhile sortie, better than most. They were laughing, covering up all the things not to think about.

'You saved my bacon there,' Peter said.

'Yeah, well, I need you around. Can't do without you, mate. Pure ego trip, saving your bacon.'

Peter smiled. He was almost, at twenty-five, a father figure to Chris. Chris could never have put into words what Peter meant to him. They had flown together since their posting in France and learned each other's ways. Not many pilots lived long enough to form such a bond. They were both aware of it but could only acknowledge it in banter. Peter was steady, a good pilot and wise tactician, while Chris was a brilliant pilot who acted out of instinct more than wisdom. Only experience and intelligence, and Peter's command, had saved him from his wilder forays up to now. Peter, unlike Chris, had never looked for excitement in his life and had a deep and unspoken admiration for Chris's natural zest, while Chris in his turn envied Peter's imperturbability under all circumstances. Their virtues complemented each other's. Together they made a formidable leadership of the squadron. But they were both acutely aware of how fleeting the partnership might be, severed either by death or by posting.

Peter came from a farming family and had been an estate manager before joining the RAF when it seemed a war was coming. So they had a bond too in the background of country life, in walking smelly spaniels through winter woods, clearing undergrowth, digging drains, watching birds through binoculars. Peter could tell any bird from its song, a skill Chris envied; he only knew them by sight. One of their greatest satisfactions was in listening together to the dawn chorus that shrilled through the woods at the edge of the airfield before the day's work started, a strange prelude to what was to come. Chris always thought that if he were shot down he would try to recall the birdsong before he died, a threnody to his departure. A last delight. One never spoke of such things, naturally, but he knew that Peter's thoughts were the same as his own.

Later, back in the mess, Chris remembered the girl again. Her face, concerned, kept coming back to him as he catnapped, waiting for the next scramble. Perhaps, if he saw her again, he would be disappointed. Yesterday was a dream, perhaps. Maybe there had been no girl at all.

It was Josie's night in the pub. The night before, Maureen had been working, and said the pilots had been there in force. Perhaps tonight they wouldn't come. Jumbo was still in London and Josie was wishing he was back, to meet her at the pub and get her feet back on the ground. It was Jumbo she loved. But all she could see was the face of his brother, the tumble of dark hair over the oily forehead, the curve of his lips in sleep. She had never thirsted for the sight of Jumbo's face in the same way, yet it was Jumbo she loved. What was wrong with her?

She watched the planes go out and come back. She did not know which was Chris's, if, indeed, he had been given another. He might be grounded. Jumbo would know which was his – they all had distinguishing letters on their sides – but Jumbo was still in London. She would have no excuse for coming out of the kitchen tonight, unless Albert the landlord let her collect the glasses. He did if he was busy.

The day seemed very long. She couldn't concentrate on painting, but went down to the lake without her paints. Some men were dismantling the broken Hurricane and loading it onto a lorry. She didn't want to be seen, and walked back through the trees, back to the lane. Restless, indecisive, she wished Jumbo were back to make her see sense. Not that she would mention what was making her so disturbed! Just to talk to him, to remind herself that she was in love with him, not Chris.

In the evening she found herself dressing carefully and studying herself in the mirror before she went to work. A touch of lipstick, her hair smoothed down, a dusting of powder over her wretched freckles ... did she look older than her sixteen years? She hoped so. She arrived at the pub early. Albert was surprised. There was no one in except two farm labourers.

'You might as well cut a few sandwiches. Those boys are always hungry, and I daresay they'll be in later.'

She started work. The sandwiches were tomato and lettuce and salad cream, the new bread difficult to cut cleanly. She couldn't think straight, listening for the sound of the racy, decrepit sports cars the airmen drove, bought for a fiver and owned by all. She was sure Chris would come in one. She knew he would come. Her hands shook. She wondered if she were sickening for something, feeling hot one minute and cold the next.

Mrs Everett, the landlord's wife, came in with some more tomatoes.

'One of them didn't come back today, they say. I don't know who it was – one of the boys who was here last night, I daresay. I don't know how they can drink and sing like they do when that happens.'

Would it be like this every night, Josie wondered, knowing one was missing?

Sick with fear. Yet she scarcely knew him.

But he came, just as her pile of sandwiches was looking like toppling. There were about a dozen of them, all very cheerful, and he was among them. They crowded round the bar and Albert started pulling pints, and she carried the sandwiches out and slid them on to the counter. She glanced up and saw Chris

105

turn away from the others and look at her. He didn't say anything, just looked, not even a smile. She could not look away, feeling the blood rushing up into her cheeks. His face was so taut, hollow-cheeked, exhausted, his glance intense, almost wild for a moment. Then, slowly, a smile.

'I wasn't sure if you were real . . . what happened yesterday. Jumbo had spoken of you . . .'

'It was strange,' she said. Was that her own voice? She could not think.

'When is Jumbo coming back?'

'I don't know.'

'Oh . . . Josie.' It was a groan, a sigh. 'What is Josie? Josephine?'

'Yes. Josephine.'

'I—'

But Albert's wife was shouting for her to bring the glasses back. She gathered a few blindly and turned away.

'I can't—'

His friend Peter came and planted a large hand on Chris's shoulder.

'Drink up, lad. You're still sober. Time is passing.' He called to Albert, 'Another pint of bitter for this thirsting youth, guv, please.'

He didn't see Josie, aware of her only as the kitchen skivvy collecting glasses, and as she scuttled back into the kitchen he led Chris back to the group. Josie was trembling. Was it her imagination or was he as disorientated in her presence as she was in his? It surely wasn't possible? No, when she glanced through the door he was laughing. His friend Peter was miming some sort of action; it was all fun and games, and Chris was not looking for her. He was lifting his glass in some sort of joking toast with the others. Mrs Everett told her to make some more sandwiches and she was then too busy to see what was happening in the bar, could only hear the singing and carousing through the door.

'Those poor lads, and one of them missing today – that nice red-haired one, the quiet one . . . I don't know how they can laugh and carry on so.' Mrs Everett was shaking her head over the washing-up. 'And our own Chris, crashing like that yesterday, so near to getting killed. I don't know how it's all going to end.'

'They're keeping the buggers at bay, that's the main thing. It all depends on them and they know it,' put in Albert.

'But they're only lads, hardly out of school.'

By the time Josie had finished her work, cleaning up and putting the glasses away, the airmen were leaving. They went out to the motley array of vehicles in the car park: two decrepit sports cars, two motorbikes and some bicycles, and Josie heard the raucous engines revving up, the laughing and shouting. She fetched her jacket, said goodnight to the publicans and went out after the vehicles had all departed. She could hear their engines fading away down the hill. It was a calm, sweet night, still warm from the soft day, scents touched off by a hint of dew. Roses and cows, earth and manure: the sky silent, waiting. Josie shivered.

Someone moved out of the porch at the front of the pub as Josie stepped onto the road.

'Josie?' The voice soft.

'What do you want?' she whispered.

'If only I knew. I want it all to stop. I want to walk home with you, and not go out in the morning. I want to take you to the lake and lie in the trees like I did yesterday, and wake up with you looking at me. I want to steal you from Jumbo.'

'He said you steal all his girls.'

'Did he? Nobody that ever mattered. He used to laugh.'

They walked along together.

'You've missed all the transport. What will you do?'

'It's called walking. I shall go across the fields, in a beeline, after I've seen you home.'

Josie laughed. He was tall beside her, his uniform smelling of cigarette smoke. He was smoking now. The red tip of the cigarette glowed in the dusk.

'How can you get up so early when you drink all night?'

'A good question. There is no choice about getting up, so get up we do. Sometimes we wish we hadn't drunk so much the night before. But when we're in the air, we're blown clean and pure and ready to start all over again. That's how it is.'

'Do you never get a day off?'

'We used to. But at the moment it's all systems go.

The weather's not helping, so perfect for invaders, everything bright and clear and easy to see. If the cloud comes down we might get a rest, but it's not forecast.'

'It seems so strange, so peaceful down here, and you up there—'

'Yes. When you come low sometimes, trying to get a Kraut off your tail, you can see them playing cricket on a village green. It's very strange.'

'I shall think of you up there.'

'When I come home I'll beat you up, show you I'm safe. How will that do?'

'What are the markings on your plane? So I can tell which is you.'

'My new one's K. K for Chris.'

'I shall look for you.'

'Yes, look for me.'

He put out his hand and took hers, and they walked in silence down the village street and into the lane that led to the farm. Josie felt as if her very blood were singing. When they got to the gate, he bent and kissed her on the lips, very gently, and whispered something, and pushed her away.

'I have to get back.' His voice was suddenly sharp and he walked quickly away, vaulted over the farm gate and disappeared through the field of cows. Josie stood transfixed. What had the whisper said? It had been choked with regret, the words reluctant. It was impossible, Josie knew it. He knew it.

She went to bed and cried. Maureen was out with

Tom, probably getting pregnant. Tom was shortly going into the army. Then Maureen would cry too, especially if she was pregnant. Josie sobbed and sobbed, for happiness, for fear, for Jumbo, for herself. And yet all the time her heart was soaring, soaring like a Hurricane into the dawn sky.

Chapter Ten

Jumbo came home the next day. Josie was lying by the lake, watching, waiting for the fighters. She had seen Hurricane K, Chris's, go out and was waiting for it to come back. She might not see it if it approached the airfield from the far side of the ridge. She knew it depended on wind direction, which way they took off and landed, but she didn't know quite how it worked. The old Hurricane had been removed; only the gouges in the grass remained where it had belly-flopped up the slope.

'I thought I'd find you here,' Jumbo said, swinging down onto the grass beside her. 'I missed you, Josie. I did miss you.'

He put his arms round her and gave her a hug and a kiss. She smiled. He was so sweet with his open, optimistic nature and laughing eyes. Nothing got him down. Even the leg.

'It was great, getting started. Jolly painful though, going by what I saw the others going through. Getting started, that is. I suppose you get used to it, hardened, after a while. Like false teeth. They just took measurements and things for me and sent me home. I have to go back in a month. Middle of September. But it's really smashing to get under way at last. I can't believe it.'

'Yes. You've been waiting so long.'

'And now Chris is here – that's a point, Josie – Ma and Pa are very upset by the fact he hasn't been up to see them yet. I've got to talk to him. I know it's only a few days and they understand how it is with him, but all the same . . . after that crash . . . they know all about it because the whole village knows, and I think he rang them to say he was OK, and they didn't say anything. But I know they're desperate to see him, very hurt if he doesn't go. He's bound to be in the pub tonight and I'll have a word with him.'

Josie hadn't told anyone but her aunt and uncle about her day in the woods with Chris asleep beside her. But she couldn't pretend to Jumbo that she hadn't met Chris: it would make life too complicated.

'I met him in the pub last night, when I was working. I had to take the sandwiches out, and he asked me if I was Josie.'

'Yes, he's heard all about you. I wrote to him and told him how my life is changed! He was bound to recognize you – I told him you were the most beautiful girl in the world, so it was obvious he would know you, wasn't it?'

Josie made herself laugh. He was so sweet! But what she had thought was love between herself and Jumbo – it was nothing, she knew now.

112

'It's your night in the pub again tonight, isn't it? I'll come down and tell Chris how the land lies. He must come up, just once at least.'

'They all look so tired – they're going out three, four times a day. Sometimes they just come back to refuel and go straight out again. I've been watching.'

'Yes. I don't know how it can go on. They've got to break the Jerries, else it will be all over with us. Hitler will invade. I pray Chris will come through. He's an ace pilot – he got chosen for the Hendon air display before all the big-wigs, to show what a plane can do, and he came down very low and flew upside down and when he landed there was grass stuck in his aerial, can you believe? So he stands a chance in that respect, not like the poor little beggars just fresh from training who get thrown right in it. The best thing would be if he got wounded a bit, not badly, but enough to keep him out of it, until it's over. My mother prays for that, I know.'

'Yes, that would be a good thing.' Josie made the obvious remark, trying to make it sound as if it meant little to her. She saw already that the path ahead was going to be extraordinarily difficult, hiding her feelings. But maybe Chris had still been suffering from concussion last night. Or she had dreamed the touch of his hand and the kiss? Or was he just a prodigious flirt? Now, with Jumbo, she was confused again.

'I'll see you tonight,' he said, as they parted. 'I love you more than ever, Josie. A few days apart – I really missed you. There's no way Chris is going to pinch this girlfriend off me, I can tell you!'

113

He gave her one of his bearlike hugs, his eyes laughing, his lips soft on her cheek and lips. He went hopping away round the lake and she turned for home, her head reeling. She had never foreseen this tangle and had no idea of how she could handle it. It was like going under water, on the way to drowning.

When Josie went to work in the pub she watched them all from the door into the kitchen, unable to keep her eyes off Chris. She noted the obvious affection between the two brothers, and Chris's bond with his section number one, Peter Palmer. She saw that Peter was slightly older and more serious than the others, his fair hair already thinning a little, his face more lined, and he wore the medal ribbons of both the DSO and the DFC below the wings on his tunic. Josie knew the two of them had been together for some time and guessed that such shared experiences had bound them close. Chris made no indication that he was aware of Josie as he drank with Peter and Jumbo, and Josie tried to stay out of the way. Albert's wife took the sandwiches in. When it came to closing time it was Jumbo who came to walk her home, and Chris went off with the others in one of the MGs, back to the airfield.

'I told him and he said he'll come home tomorrow, instead of going to the pub. I think his pal Peter is coming too, and how about you as well, Josie? You're not in the pub tomorrow, are you? I know Ma would like to see you again. Make it a bit of a dinner party.'

'Is that how your mother wants it? Not just Chris alone?'

'It's how Chris wants it. He said about you coming too. He doesn't want it just family. I know why. I know exactly why.'

Josie didn't quite know what he meant but did not enquire further. She saw that having such tough parents as the brothers did was something of a burden. The likes of Auntie Betty would have suited them better in the circumstances: unquestioning, homely, showing nothing but all-enveloping love and kindness. She suspected that Chris and Jumbo had something to live up to in face of their parents. But did Chris want her there because he wanted to see her again, or to make the buffer between him and his parents, along with Peter Palmer? She didn't know and couldn't guess.

She dressed with care the following evening, very nervous. She was going to be out of her depth, with no experience of dinner parties, quite apart from her fraught relationships with the two brothers. She must try not to put a foot wrong, keep her head down. But not appear a ninny in front of Chris! Impossible to get it right, she feared. But dear Jumbo came to meet her, swinging down the road in the warm evening, dressed in his best suit and wearing a tie.

'We should have arranged for Chris to pick you up – we didn't think! But if he's bringing Pete – his car's only a two-seater – although they get at least six in – or on – it when they come to the pub. At least he'll take you home, don't worry.'

Jumbo was obviously not worried about anything.

His mother had had Tilly the housekeeper at work making the mostly unused dining room look respectable, for the table was laid with shining silver and sparkling glasses, the chairs cleared of piles of *Horse and Hound* and *The Field* and the dog hairs swept from the carpets. Mrs Patterson was wearing a dress, expensive at one time, Josie guessed, but now looking more comfortable than smart.

'How nice to see you again, Josie,' she said smoothly. 'My husband will be down in a minute. You didn't meet him before, did you? He's only just got home from London. He works a very long day.'

As she spoke a man, very tall and erect, came down the stairs, trailed by two labradors. He had an undoubtedly authoritative bearing, and his blindness was not obvious in his looks apart from the eyes – dark blue like Chris's – not moving; the nose was Wellingtonian, slightly hooked, and the lips still sweet and curved, again like Chris's.

'Josie is here, dear, Jumbo's girlfriend,' said Mrs Patterson. 'But not Chris and Peter. I'm sure they won't be long. Josie, this is my husband, Archie.'

She put her hand on Josie's elbow and nudged her towards the blind man, who held out his hand for her to shake.

'I'm delighted to meet you, Josie.' His voice was crisp and cool.

Josie thought that this was a man you wouldn't dare

argue with. She stammered her how-do-you-do and was relieved that the eyes could not rake her over, as his wife's had done on their first meeting. Any conversation was then interrupted by the super-charged engine of the airmen's MG charging across the gravel outside and the sound of a long, satisfying skid to halt.

'Ah, the boys are here!'

Mrs Patterson went to run out, then seemed to hold herself in check and stopped in the doorway, cool.

'Chris! At last!' Her voice quivered.

Josie watched Chris run up the steps and embrace her. She offered her cheek. There were tears in her eyes.

'Oh, Chris!'

Josie ached for her, seeing herself in the woman, agonizing for Chris's safety. But one did not speak of these things.

'Dad!'

They shook hands, no embrace, but the blind man's face radiated joy. Peter was introduced: 'My number one, my one and only – I've spoken of him many times but I don't think you've met him before.'

More handshakes, and then Mrs Patterson said to Chris, 'And have you met Josie, Jumbo's girlfriend?'

Chris had to look at her.

'Josie? Yes, we met in the pub, with Jumbo.'

Josie could not meet his eyes. She felt her wretched cheeks flaming. Would Jumbo see?

'What will you boys drink? Mother found a bottle of champagne in the cellar – don't you think this calls for champagne? So long since we saw you, Chris, and so rare for us to be all together.'

The colonel went to the sideboard, opened the champagne like a sighted person, and poured it into the glasses. Josie noticed how his hands groped, but so expertly, feeling what his eyes could not see, so practised and smooth. His pride made it so, she guessed. Not to give way. They took the glasses.

'Here. A celebration! To you both, to stay safe, and to Jumbo's new leg!'

Josie had never had champagne before. She had vowed to drink as little as possible, fearing it would loosen her tongue, but loved the icy, bubbly feel of it in her mouth. It made her hiccup. Jumbo laughed.

'Here's to us, Josie,' he whispered. 'Blow them.'

The dogs were ecstatic to see Chris and fawned over him feverishly, and he got down on his knees and cuddled and kissed them.

'They haven't forgotten you! And yet they've scarcely seen you for ages – how loyal animals are!'

'Better than humans, you always said, Ma.' Chris got up, grinning.

'They don't give you grief,' she said, but with a smile.

'No grief today! The family all together,' said the colonel. 'We've missed you, Chris – so long! But we understand how it is. I understand. Let's hope things will ease up soon, when we get them on the run. We're not short of planes any longer, only well-trained pilots, I believe.'

118

'Yes, the poor kids have only done eighty hours solo, half of them. Or less. No fighting experience at all. If they survive the first sorties the bright ones learn how to keep out of trouble – a strong sense of self-preservation helps. We've all got that, after all.'

'Let's sit down. Tilly's made us a good meal. John Abbot lost a young heifer last week – got stuck in a ditch – so we've all had a nice present. If we didn't have the poultry in the yard and a few farmers' gifts, we'd be pretty hungry on the rations we get.' Mrs Patterson completely accepted the privilege of the upper classes and Chris and Peter had more tact than to tell her that the whole air force lived mostly on baked beans. Josie could see how difficult it was for the pilots to relate to this calm, orderly life, happening just down the road from their fraught, nerve-shredding existence. She knew exactly why Chris hadn't wanted to come.

But the dinner was delicious; even Auntie Betty's good cooking could not vie with Tilly pulling all the stops out to feed the dear boys. She waited on them, dressed in her best flowered pinny. Chris got up and hugged her when she came in and Tilly cried unashamedly, the tears running down her cheeks. Josie could see that this embarrassed Mrs Patterson, who asked her rather sharply to bring the large serving spoon from the dresser. Jumbo hopped up and fetched it, kind as ever, and Tilly apologized and backed away. Josie was sitting opposite Chris and Peter, next to Jumbo, and tried to keep her eyes down, desperate not to give away her feelings. But it was hard not to feast upon the features opposite, not to hang upon his every word, every fleeting expression; she was drawn as if to a magnet. He did not look at her or include her in the conversation at all, but the talk was mainly between the colonel and the two airmen, about the war and politics. Nobody spoke of what the two men did every day, although Chris's prang was mentioned and Chris described his amazement at ending up in his childhood playground in such an unexpected fashion. Then he said, 'I must have passed out after I got out, in the wood somewhere, because I didn't come to till evening. Then I walked back.' No mention of Josie, no glance between them. Her heart thudded. She stared at her plate. Perhaps she had dreamed it after all.

She heard the colonel say, 'They have started bombing airfields – I think it's the strategy now, to ground the opposition before it gets into the sky. Have you got shelters up there?'

'Yes,' said Chris. 'But we've got to get the planes off before they arrive, so we're not likely to hang around in shelters. We get some warning, with luck. It's you who might need a shelter here, and the village too. They aren't brilliant at hitting their targets.'

'Biggin Hill's been hit, and Manston's been wiped out several times,' said Peter. 'But they're ace at filling in the holes. None of them have been out of operation for more than a few hours. We've got to have somewhere to come home to, after all.'

'There's always the lawn up at the manor,' Jumbo said.

They laughed. No one would have suspected, Josie thought, that it was anything that mattered at all.

Then they talked about what was showing in the London theatres, and how the fighter pilots liked nothing better than a night out, dancing and drinking in a West End club, driving home in the small hours to catch the dawn flights.

'A good night's sleep would do you more good,' Mrs Patterson said.

'A typical mother's view!'

The evening broke up comparatively early, Chris using a good night's sleep as an excuse to leave. His mother could hardly argue.

'We can run Josie back too, if she sits on my lap,' Chris said. 'Save her a walk. It's hardly out of our way.'

'Come again soon, darling. We see so little of you these days.'

'OK. Tell us when the next heifer falls in a ditch and we'll be down. Tell Tilly it was a wizard meal. Thanks, Ma, for everything – it's great to be home again. And don't worry about us too much.'

'You never gave us a quiet life even before all this happened. I think we're getting used to it, your father and I.'

They went out into the warm dusk. Peter took the driver's seat and Chris got in beside him.

'Come on, Josie.' He held out his arms. 'Be my darling. Or else you'll have to walk.'

They all laughed and Josie slipped onto Chris's lap.

Jumbo shut the door on them. Peter revved up the engine. Josie had a glimpse of the parents standing arm in arm in the portico, smiling bravely, Jumbo laughing, and then they were hurtling away down the drive, gravel spraying.

'To the pub, for God's sake,' Chris said to Peter, in a different, desperate voice. 'God, it's like play-acting in front of them, pretending you're sane.'

Josie felt his hard thighs under her, squashed tight in the little bucket seat. His arm squeezed her shoulder.

'Was it awful for you, Josie, being on your best behaviour? You were perfect, keeping cool. They aren't very easy, my parents, are they?'

'I think they're very nice.'

'Yes, they are, that's the problem. Nothing to kick against. One feels a heel.'

'Oh come on, Chris, they're bloody proud of you,' Peter said. 'That day we got our gongs at the palace – when the king was talking to you – you should have seen their faces! They couldn't hide it then. You're their blue-eyed boy.'

'Yeah, but it's easier kissing Tilly than my mother. She brought us up really. Ask Jumbo.'

'She's a bloody fine cook!'

'The meal was wizard, yes. She ought to be employed at base.'

'If only!'

'God, if only the weather would close down we might get a rest. Some time to eat, eh! And sleep. I could sleep for ever!'

'You said you were going back to sleep,' Josie pointed out, as they skidded to a halt outside the pub. 'Now you're going to the pub.'

'Peter's going to the pub,' Chris said. 'I'm taking you home.'

'OK,' said Peter affably. 'See you later.'

He slid out of the driving seat and Chris moved over, Josie taking the passenger seat to herself. Chris drove away immediately, but steadily, heading through the village and into the lane that led to Josie's cottage. But before they got to the cottage, he pulled into a gateway and turned off the engine. It was hardly dark, the stars scarcely visible, but a new moon shining brightly.

Chris looked at it and said, 'It would be magical up there now, Josie. You can't imagine, from here, how beautiful. I would like to fly away and never come back.'

'You must come back! I look for you all the time.'

'We're living in a dream. Half dream, half nightmare. There's no in-between. I don't know how it can pan out. I scarcely know you, yet I think about you all the time. What's happening? God alone knows.'

He put out his arm and pulled her close.

'It's not fair on you.'

'Fair doesn't matter,' she whispered.

'I've never thought of anyone before like I think of you.'

Josie lifted her face to his. She moved involuntarily; she couldn't stop herself. He bent and kissed her. She

123

could feel his heart beating, pressed so close. She felt almost faint with the emotion that flooded her, loving him with this animal passion that she could scarcely recognize as part of her nature. What was happening to her? He kissed her lips and her ears and her throat and stroked her hair.

'I love you, Josie.'

'I love you.'

'But it's impossible.' He groaned softly, still kissing her. 'It's impossible,' he whispered.

He pushed her away. 'We should have gone to the pub, stayed with Peter. He's used to saving my life.'

Josie could see the dark hump of the cottage up the lane. Maureen and Tom could easily come by, she knew. But . . . 'Why is it impossible?'

'Because of . . . because I've got no future. There is no future. I don't want you hurt.'

He started the car engine.

'Maybe, Josie, afterwards. If there is an afterwards. But there's Jumbo. I've destroyed Jumbo's life once. I can't do it again.'

He drove out of the gateway.

Josie was confused. 'I will be hurt. You can't change that. It's too late. I can't help it.'

'No. I'm a fool, I should know better. I'm sorry, Josie.'

'But you said you loved me.'

'Yes. I'm not such a fool as to take that back. I love you.'

Josie's heart soared. She didn't know whether she

was laughing or crying. She knew he couldn't, wouldn't, stay away, whatever he said now. It wasn't possible. She had a crazy image of herself racing across the airfield, chasing his Hurricane with the K on the side, and the Hurricane coming towards her, looking for her as it came home. It must always come home!

'Goodnight, darling Josie,' he said.

He leaned across and opened her door. 'Hop out. Look cool. Take the stars out of your eyes, else Auntie Betty will see. And me too. It never happened!'

'It did!'

He laughed. 'It did, yes. You're a smasher, Josie.'

He drove away. Josie stood watching as the unlit car disappeared round the bend between the hedges. It was ten minutes before she felt calm enough to go indoors.

Chapter Eleven

Josie heard the Hurricanes taking off while she was in the vegetable garden picking a lettuce for lunch. There was something different from usual, the racket of their engines mixed with another, hardly discernible engine noise coming from the south. She straightened up and saw a formation of bombers etched clear against the blue sky, the pencil shape of Dornier 111s looking exactly like the pictures in her recognition books. They were aiming straight for the airfield and, as she watched in disbelief, she heard the unmistakable whistle of falling bombs.

'Auntie Betty!' she screamed.

She actually saw the bombs coming, black dots hurtling in a string from the leading bomber. She flung herself down beside the garden shed and put her arms over her head. So this is what it was to be bombed! The noise of the explosions was excruciating. The ground shook and she heard earth pattering down on the shed roof. She knew they were bombing – or trying to bomb – the airfield and hopefully the planes on the ground, but most of the Hurricanes were away. She lifted her head and saw them skimming up into the sky. Another bomber released its load, this time more accurately, and then another. The air resounded to the awful whistle of falling bombs; explosions rocked the ground. Uncle Bert's cows went galloping past at the bottom of the garden, their tails in the air, and dogs barked all over the village. Yet the sun still shone serenely, there were no bleeding bodies, only – presumably – large holes in the airfield. Also, all over the surrounding landscape.

The bombers had divided, some continuing and some turning for home, no longer in formation. They were now being harassed by fighters. The noise of the air battle reverberated across the landscape, the sharp rattle of fire mixed with the scream of engines at full throttle. Josie watched, mesmerized, aware only of Chris – perhaps – up there in danger of his life. She felt herself shaking. She realized Auntie Betty was standing beside her, white-faced.

'I hope nothing's happened to Bert!'

They both stared up at the sky, but the action was quickly dispersed, and in a few moments there was nothing to be seen, save aircraft like gnats glittering far away in the sunlight.

'Well I never!' They were both shaken, Auntie Betty trembling. 'Fancy, right out here!'

'It's the airfield. But the planes got away, I saw them. They wanted to smash them up on the ground. I read it in the paper. It's their new idea.'

But now, suddenly, a bomber appeared coming back, low, smoke trailing from one of its engines.

Auntie Betty grabbed Josie's arm. 'Oh my Gawd, I hope he's not landing here!'

Above it two Hurricanes swooped in, followed by two Messerschmitt 109s, and suddenly the sky was full of aircraft again, the acrobatics hard to follow. The Hurricanes were intent on finishing off the bomber, the Messerschmitts intent on getting the Hurricanes. Josie and her aunt stood hard against the shed as if paralysed. The action took place in seconds, right over their heads.

It was so quick Josie hardly took it in. She knew the Hurricanes were Chris and Peter by the letters on their fuselages. One of them – hard to say which – went in for a finishing burst on the bomber and the other spun round and went head-on for the 109, which was about to put a burst into the attacking Hurricane. It seemed like a suicidal move but the 109's attention was on the other plane and he was too late to see the attack from the side, which blew him apart. The attacking Hurricane veered violently in the explosion, and as it did so it received a devastating burst of fire from the other German fighter. It shuddered, then rolled away and up and round like a demented fly to get its attacker back in its sights, but now the remaining German was diving for home, throttle wide open, and the damaged Hurricane could not get near enough for his fire to be effective. The air was full of bits of flaming aeroplane and black smoke and the smell of cordite. The bomber was going down now, plunging sharply with both engines on fire, and the remaining three fighters were chasing seaward. But the 109 had the legs of the Hurricanes and after several bursts of farewell fire they gave up the chase, rolled over side by side and headed back, mission accomplished. They both trailed white glycol and were spattered with holes in wings and fuselage but they were still flying, coming in to land. Whether they could find a path to land in amongst the smoking bomb craters was another matter.

Josie and her aunt meanwhile were shaking at the sight of carnage all round them. The bomber was burning fiercely in the cow field a couple of hundred yards away and bits of the fighter were all over the place, the tail plane stuck upright in the golden stubble where Josie had lately been toiling and one wing lying on top of one of Uncle Bert's haystacks. Where the pilot was to be found neither of the women wanted to know. Pigs were squealing with excitement from the farm and the same herd of cows was still on the gallop at the bottom of the field.

'Oh my Gawd, Gawd save us!' Auntie Betty wept. She was nearly fainting and Josie put her arms round her to hold her up. They held onto each other, trying to get themselves together.

Then Betty said, 'The poor boys! The poor boys!' and burst into tears.

'But they're Germans, Auntie! They tried to kill our boys, and us too. They hit the airfield and there's

129

lots of people working up there. They'll be dead too.'

They didn't kill Chris! she thought. Having seen it with her own eyes, she couldn't believe that that was what he did all day, he and his roistering, drinking friends in the pub – kill or be killed, duelling in the sky. Had he got down safely? Smoke was rising from the airfield and they could hear the firefighters' bells ringing. Already some men were running across the field towards the burning bomber and an air force lorry was screaming down the lane towards the gateway where she and Chris had stopped last night. She was drawn to watch, morbidly, going down to the fence and climbing over it into the field. Were these men in the bomber men that Chris, or mild-mannered Peter, had killed before her very eyes? It seemed impossible, knowing them. Yet this was the truth of war. This was the first time it had come close.

As she stood there she saw the air force lorry pull up sharply and the men shouted to the farm boys still running towards the plane. Even as they shouted the plane's petrol tanks exploded and a huge burst of flame leaped into the air. Josie felt the heat slamming into her, stopping her in her tracks. She heard herself scream. One of the Germans who had staggered out of the plane was blown into the air, arms and legs cartwheeling against the sky, and a great pall of black smoke belched out across the landscape, evil and stinking.

Men leaped from the lorry and ran towards the flaming pyre. The farm boys and the Germans were all lying still in the grass, the cows bellowing distractedly from the bottom of the field.

Josie did not wait to see any more. She turned back to the house and climbed back into the garden, but as she did so she heard a shout from behind and saw that two of the men off the lorry were coming up the field after her, half-dragging the German survivor, barely conscious, between them.

'Can we dump 'im 'ere, gel, till the military come and get 'im? We've got a lot to do. These blokes'll guard 'im for yer.'

They threw the man bodily over the fence into the garden. The blokes to guard over him were Tom and another farm boy, the ones blown off their feet by the explosion, now recovered and looking goggle-eyed with excitement and importance.

'He won't be putting up a fight, by the look of 'im,' the man said, unnecessarily. 'Don't be too bothered about making the bastard comfortable. You should see what they've done up on the airfield.'

They went back across the field to join their mates, whose job it was to recover the rest of the German crew, dead or alive, from the bomber. Dead, not alive, Josie was convinced. The man at her feet must be the only survivor. The three of them, joined shortly by a quivering Auntie Betty, stood looking at him. They were all still in a state of shock and nobody made a move. Josie could only take in that the boy at her feet was beautiful, very young, the sort of man that, by sight, she would instinctively want to be friends with.

131

But he was a German and Chris or Peter had killed all his companions and nearly him as well.

Auntie Betty said with a quaver in her voice, 'Well, poor lad, he's some mother's son, German or no.'

Tom kicked him. 'Bloody Kraut.'

'That's enough!' Auntie Betty's voice was sharp. 'Get his helmet off now, and his boots, and I'll fetch a couple of blankets and a pillow. I think he's coming round.'

'We ought to tie him up,' said Tom's companion.

'Don't be stupid,' said Josie scathingly. 'He's hardly going anywhere, is he?'

She was calming down now, with something to do. The airman's eyes were open, as blue as the sky, looking round in bewilderment.

'You're a prisoner, mate,' said Tom. 'No home fires burning for you.'

'Oh, shut up,' said Josie. She had learned some German at school, and said some comforting words to the boy, that he was all right and would be looked after. Not that all the rest of his crew were dead.

Tom stared at her. 'Blimey, whose side are you on?'

'Meine Freunde?' the boy muttered.

'Your friends?' Josie shrugged. It was impossible. She could see across the field that the men could still not get near the inferno, and half-suspected that she could smell burning flesh.

He could tell the truth by her face. Tears trickled out of his eyes.

'Blimey, what a twerp,' said Tom.

Josie turned on him. 'Go away! We don't want you here if that's all the help you can give. Go and look after your blooming cows. They need you.'

'All right. Keep your hair on! You can have him. But if he gets up and beats you to a pulp you've only yourselves to blame.'

'Don't be so ridiculous!'

Josie was glad to see the backs of the two boys as they went away towards the burning bomber. Half the village was out there now to look, and more air force personnel arrived to take charge and herd them out of the way. But it was too much to expect to stop them seeing the gruesome removal of the charred bodies. Josie shuddered. Their German survivor, lying amongst the cabbages and lettuces, could not see what was going on, Uncle Bert's compost heap blocking out the view, but he could hear the commotion, and smell and hear his bomber's demise.

He muttered something else, still crying.

'Crikey, he should still be in school,' Auntie Betty said. 'Lie still, dear, don't move. I'll make you a cup of tea.'

But before it was boiled a military ambulance came down the lane and some men got out carrying a stretcher.

'Where is he, love?'

They loaded him up, very professional, brusque but not ungentle, and in a few moments they had driven away. Betty and Josie stood staring after the ambulance, still shaken, then Auntie Betty said, 'I must go out and see if Bert's OK down at the farm, and then we can walk up to the village and see what's what, where those bombs fell. I hope no one was hurt. What about up the big house and your friend Jumbo? Lucky Maureen was working over at Stratton's this morning and there weren't no bombs in that direction.'

It hadn't occurred to Josie to be frightened for Jumbo, only Chris, and she acknowledged this now with a lurch of shame, for the Patterson house had certainly been in the line of the falling bombs.

'We don't want to join those ghouls out there,' her aunt said, nodding out to the field. But then she noticed one of the ghouls was Bert, admittedly on the edge of the crowd on his way back to the cottage, so she gave him a wave and he came over and they exclaimed over the morning's happenings.

'Blown our nice ricks all over the place and there's a huge hole now in Long Meadow, right where the beet's to go in, and all the fencing down against the wood.'

Betty gave him a lecture on farmland not mattering a tinker's cuss compared with poor dead people all around them, including Germans, so Bert went back to the bomber and Josie hurried with her down to the village, where everyone was out, chattering nineteen to the dozen. She could see from the village street that the Patterson house was still standing serenely in the sunshine so she presumed Jumbo was all right, but all she could think of was whether Chris was able to land

134

safely on the stricken airfield. All was mayhem up there, with vehicles to-ing and fro-ing. Two Hurricanes came in to land, wheels down, but after flying low over the field they turned away and disappeared towards some more welcoming home. Had Chris and Peter done the same? Josie hadn't seen them since the bomber crashed. But they had both been damaged, and perhaps not able to fly farther. She was worried. Sitting on the churchyard wall, she watched the women gossiping all round her. It seemed no one had been hurt, although the bombs had landed indiscriminately, only a few on their intended target.

'Useless gits,' was the general opinion. 'Serve 'em right, those ones that got frizzled up there.'

Certainly the happening had stirred the village like a stick in a wasps' nest: everyone was out, most of them now drifting out up the lane to stare at the bomber. The smell of its burning and the pall of smoke still hung in the sky. Josie found she was still getting the shivers from the shock of it, and neighbours were respectful – she had been so close. Auntie Betty was starting to enjoy her new celebrity, having the survivor in her garden. Some said she should have put the garden fork through him and she was getting het up about it. Josie slipped down and wandered away, and met Jumbo swinging up across the field.

'Josie! Thank goodness you're not hurt! And Chris, did you see him? Cripes, we were all in a stew up there, right over our heads!'

'Did he get down OK?' She tried to sound casual.

'Yes, I went up to see. I don't know how they did it, mind you – there's craters everywhere. But they had to, didn't they – they were both all shot up. As far as I know they're OK though. Ma rang through. She was a bit fraught, for her. She can pull rank when she has to, I can tell you – the colonel's wife and all that. She doesn't often lose her cool.'

'No. I saw it all. It was amazing, terrible.'

'Well, they're probably in the mess now having a cup of tea. Maybe they'll have the rest of the day off, the planes all ripped up and nowhere to take off. They might come over. Or sleep, I suppose.'

'I don't know how you can go to sleep, after that.'

'No. Chris has nightmares, I know that. I've heard him.'

Josie was silent. She found it hard, thinking of Chris, relating to Jumbo. She felt ashamed.

She told Jumbo about the German boy.

'I couldn't really think of him as the enemy when he was lying there. I felt sorry for him, more than anything.'

'I know. It's weird. When Chris shot a Jerry down once, the pilot landed by parachute quite nearby and they had him in the pub in the evening, before he was carted off to prison, and gave him a really good time. Chris said he was an ace pilot and they'd had a great fight. They used to do that. But later, Chris lost a pal – he was coming down by parachute and a German fighter came and shot him up and killed him, and since then, it's been different. Kill the bastards,

136

whatever. Although, in spite of saying that, I don't think Chris has ever shot a Jerry on a parachute.'

'Do you think he'll be in the pub tonight?' She tried not to ask the question but couldn't help herself.

'Yes, I expect so. You're on tonight, aren't you?'

'Yes.'

'I'll see you there, then. I'd better go back because of Ma. I said I'd report on things over here. She was worried about you. Me too.' He grinned. 'I don't want you in little pieces. I like you as you are.'

He gave her a hug and a kiss.

'I'll come back with you up the lane and have a look at the bomber while I'm about it.'

'Was it Chris or Peter who shot it down?'

'Oh, both, I should think. They work together, watch each other's backs.'

Over a belated lunch Auntie Betty said that if the airfield was going to be bombed Josie was hardly in a safe place any more.

'I'll write to your mother and see what she thinks about it. You may be safer at home.'

Josie stopped herself from crying out in horror. She didn't want to go home!

She swallowed her alarm and tried to say calmly, 'It's as bad down there. Mum said they'd had bombs quite near.'

'Well, these are directed right at the airfield, which is very close. She just gets random ones when they don't know where they are, or they're being shot at.'

'Eh, what's the difference?' said Bert. 'If your

137

number's on it, that's it. Even a bloody cow. I reckon we won't get much milk for a day or two, that bit of excitement.'

'Even so, Josie, it wouldn't hurt for you to go home for a few days and see your mother. She misses you, I know.'

'A few days?' She could bear that. Just.

But a few days later the airfield was bombed again. The Hurricanes had been moved to a hidden airfield nearby and not a single plane was damaged. But Uncle Bert was hit by a flying tile off the end of the cowshed and had to go to hospital to be stitched up, and Auntie Betty insisted that Josie must go home.

'I can't be responsible for you here! You've only got to read the papers!'

They were full of the might of the German assault and the ferocious resistance being put up by the fighter force. It was a crucial time: the Germans were beginning to show signs of desperation, having expected the enemy to cave in quietly seeing their own strength was so overpowering. But time and time again their bomber squadrons were broken up by the British fighters and sent ignominiously off course or down in flames. The morale of their air force plummeted. As Chris pointed out, 'It's no joke fighting so far from home, knowing there's the Channel to cross when you're damaged. It was like that for us over Dunkirk.' He had only had a week's leave since the spring. But at the height of the battle he was not hopeful of getting more. Josie knew the papers did not dwell on the deaths of the British pilots, but with her own eyes she saw the changing clientele in the pub at night-time. She knew Chris and Peter were leading charmed lives. She knew that to love Chris was to self-destruct. There was nowhere to go.

'I love you, oh, I love you so!' She could not help herself, one night after they left the pub. He kissed her passionately. They could hear the others leaving, shouting and singing.

'Auntie Betty's sending me home! I've got to go!'

'Tell her I'll take you. I'll take you myself.'

'How! How can you?'

'In the evening, when we're finished, I'll take you to London. We'll have a night on the town, you and me, and then I'll deliver you, and be back here in time for duty. No one will ever know if we make a detour. We'll live it up, Josie!'

'Is it possible?'

'Yes, we used to do it when we weren't so tired. I've got to go. They're waiting for me. But this time, with you, Josie, yes, we'll do it. Tell your auntie, tomorrow or the day after, whenever. I will take you.'

Auntie Betty had already looked up the train timetable and written that her sister should expect Josie. When she got in Josie told her that she was getting a lift with Chris Patterson.

'Chris? You mean the pilot, Jumbo's brother?'

'Yes.'

Auntie Betty was dumbfounded. 'But – how can . . . ? I don't understand . . .'

'They go down to the West End to a nightclub. He's going to deliver me on the way, save me going on the train.'

'Yeah, I've heard of it,' put in Uncle Bert. 'That's what they do, these fighter boys. Live it up in the West End, dancing and all that.'

'Not with Josie!'

'No, just the lift.' Josie, who rarely lied, felt terrible. But desperate. She would go, whatever Auntie Betty said.

'It's on the way, Wimbledon.'

Luckily Auntie Betty's grasp of London's geography was very vague so she didn't argue, and Bert said, 'Nice, in that little MG. I wouldn't mind that ride myself.'

'Well, you tell him no speeding, and no getting drunk in the pub first. I'll tell him, before you go. Not to drive like he's in his aeroplane. When's he taking you?'

'He said tomorrow, or whenever I'm ready.'

'Well, you'd better pack your things. Have you told Albert?'

'I'll tell him. And Jumbo.'

But whatever was she to say to Jumbo? She had to go over to Nightingales to see him. She had to tell him. But what to tell him? That Chris was giving her a lift home, no more? She knew she had to tell him the truth, but could not bear it. There must be a way of fudging it somehow.

She trudged up the drive to the big house, filled

with dread. She told herself she had just come to tell Jumbo that she was going home, and that Chris was giving her a lift to Wimbledon, no more. She didn't have to say any more. If Jumbo was going to say how much he would miss her . . . well, she could pretend something, somehow . . . how much she would miss him.

The front door was open as usual but she rang the old-fashioned, jangling bell that hung on a chain. A flurry of barking dogs came racing down the hall and behind them Jumbo, swinging on his crutches.

'Hey, Josie! Guess what!'

Before Josie could utter a word he spilled out his news.

'In the post – today – my letter came! I'm to go down to the hospital tomorrow! Can you believe it? At once. No more waiting. My leg's ready!'

'Oh Jumbo, that's super! How wonderful!'

'I can't believe it! I thought it would be ages yet. I can't tell you how I feel – oh, it's just wizard! I was coming over to tell you.'

His expression then changed and he looked at her anxiously. 'There's nothing wrong, is there, that you've come up here . . . ?' She never visited his house ordinarily. 'You couldn't have heard? I've only just found out myself.'

'No. I came up to tell you that I'm going home. Auntie Betty insists. I don't want to go, so I'll try and make it just a few days.'

'When are you going?'

'I'm not sure. Tomorrow perhaps, or the next day.'

'Well that's good timing, isn't it? If you've got to go, and I'm going to the hospital, it's a good thing it's happening at the same time. Maybe you'll be able to visit me – we won't be far apart. I'm going down there with my father, when he goes to work. His chauffeur's going to drop me off. I should think he could take you too, if it suits you. Even if you have to get off with me, you'd only have a bit of a tube ride to Wimbledon.'

For a moment Josie wondered if that was what she would do. It would be better, delivering her to sanity. Her head told her clearly that she only had to nod and accept Jumbo's plan, and she would have nothing else to worry about. It was so simple. She opened her mouth but the words would not come out.

'I – I—' She floundered. She couldn't! And in that moment she realized that courage wasn't only about fighting Germans hand to hand: it was having the strength to face facts. She didn't love Jumbo any more. He had to know.

'Chris is taking me down,' she said. 'He's promised.'

'Chris! How can he? You mean after dark?'

'Yes.'

She saw the change come over Jumbo's face as the implication sank in. The sun went in as the cloud covered it. She could see his mind turning it over, drinking in the disappointment. More than disappointment.

'He used to do that, after a day's fighting. They all did. They'd go to a dance hall, drink and eat and pick up girls and dance. Is that what he's doing? Or is he just taking you to your mother and handing you over? He's not, is he? Not until he's danced with you and kissed you and made love to you?'

To have it spelt out, what they were going to do, was terrible. Josie felt almost faint at facing Jumbo's bitterness. In a few seconds his sweet, open, happy face had changed to an almost unrecognizable mask of anger and pain. His voice was rough and choked.

'Again! Chris again! Always – always – my brother, who thinks he loves me. He takes my girls and it's always been a joke. Until now. But it isn't a joke now, not with you, Josie. I've seen it coming. I'm not blind.'

He made no attempt to appeal to her. He backed away as if he could not stand the sight of her. She would rather have had to argue, she realized, as the only platitude that came to her lips stumbled stupidly into the abyss: 'I didn't mean it to happen!'

'That's what he always said, and I laughed. He laughed. But this time it's different. Well, go with him, Josie, and I hope it will make you happy, but I don't think the pain of loving someone who might be killed at any moment will give you much joy.'

He turned abruptly and went crutching away into the house. His reaction was so quick and final that Josie was left stunned. She had expected the outburst, but with Jumbo, so kind and intelligent, she had expected to be drawn into a mire of reasoning and entreaty. It was as if he had hit her. She stood forlornly, her tenderness towards poor Jumbo bringing the tears to her eyes, along with an undeniable lurch of self-pity.

His parting words were only too true. Did he truly think she had not realized the terrible cost to herself of her love? Why was she doing it to herself after all the pleasure of the days when she thought she was in love with Jumbo? Because she couldn't help it, was the answer. She just couldn't help herself.

She turned and stumbled away down the drive. Jumbo's acute reaction had felled her. She went home and flung herself into a frenzy of gardening, clearing the hedgerow and making a bonfire, working herself stupid so as to stop herself thinking. She wanted the contents of her brain on the bonfire along with the dead branches and leaves, to scorch it clean, exorcize her infidelity. But in the evening she had to go down to the pub, it was her night on. She had to see Chris to find out which day he was taking her.

When he came into the bar she went out to him, like a moth to a candle. He came away from his pals, a pint in his hand.

'We'll go tomorrow,' he said, 'if it suits you.'

'Yes. Tomorrow.'

He smiled into her eyes. 'We'll have a great evening, Josie. Don't look so scared!'

'I told Jumbo you were taking me.'

His expression changed.

'What did he say?'

'That we were going to eat and drink and dance and make love and that you always stole his girlfriends.'

'Oh, Christ!' A look of despair came over his face. 'You shouldn't have told him, Josie!'

'I couldn't help it, because he said he was going to London for his leg and I could have a lift with him in his father's car.'

'I can't bear to do this to him!'

'You don't have to.'

'I can't help myself, Josie. I could be dead tomorrow, and for that very reason I want to do this. I want to hold you in my arms, Josie, away from this place, away from fighting and killing and being scared shitless – Jumbo doesn't know what it's like. He's no idea how gutless I really am. That I can do this to him – the worst thing ever. He doesn't understand what makes me do it – I don't understand myself how I can do this to him . . .'

Josie was frightened by this rambling, almost incoherent speech from the ultra-cool Chris. She felt she was a helpless twig being swirled down a flooding waterfall, quite incapable of action or thought. If Chris didn't understand what he was doing, she was sure she didn't either.

Then he seemed to pull himself together, and started to make sense.

'Tell Jumbo, if it pleases him, that next week I'm getting leave and then the squadron's being posted. We're being taken out for a rest. I shall be going away and I shan't see you again. Jumbo will have a clear field. And for this reason we're going to have a great night out in London, you and me, and damn Jumbo. We'll go tomorrow, that's a date.'

'Chris!'

'I'll call for you as soon as I can. About seven, with luck.'

Albert was shouting at her to bring the glasses. She had no chance to speak to him again. All she had now was tomorrow, and after that . . . she could not believe it. Like coming to the edge of a cliff and falling off. She went home early, pleading a headache, afraid she was going to start crying and would never stop.

When she went to bed that night Maureen, putting her hair in curlers, asked her if it was true that she was going to London with Chris.

'Yes, he's taking me home. He offered. How do you know?' Was nothing a secret in this incestuous village? But no, of course, her parents had told her. She was fast forgetting the sequence of events. Probably everybody knew already that Jumbo loved her and she loved Chris and Jumbo's leg had come . . .

She waited angrily for Maureen to ask more questions, but she said nothing for a while. Then, 'We saw you. Tom and I, we saw you.'

'What do you mean?'

'In his car, up the lane. In the gateway. I thought Jumbo was your boyfriend. Are you two-timing him? It looked like it, the way you were.'

'Yes. But Jumbo knows now. I didn't want it to happen! I can't help it.'

Maureen laughed, rather unkindly. 'It's all right for some, I suppose, having a choice.'

Josie said angrily, 'Chris is being posted. The

146

squadron's moving away, so that's the end of that, if you're so interested.'

Faced with Maureen's lugubrious presence, hardly a shoulder to cry on, Josie suddenly yearned for her old friend Mary and their Biggles talk – how Mary would understand her feelings! Perhaps, going home, she would find Mary there – what bliss, if she did! Her muddled allegiances were hard to bear alone, she realized that suddenly. She felt a surge of nostalgia for the old innocent giggly days, hiding in the school boiler room and talking about stupid things. It seemed an age ago now, when she was a child. Loving Chris, so close to death every day – there was nothing childish any more in her thoughts.

Maureen said, 'Tom's joined up. He's going away soon.'

Her voice faltered. Josie suddenly saw her looking very young and frightened.

'And I think I'm pregnant.'

'Maureen!'

Maureen burst into tears and Josie found herself sitting on the bed with her arms round her, saying stupidly, 'Don't cry, don't cry!'

'I don't know what to do!' Maureen wailed.

Josie thought: That makes two of us! Poor Maureen! She had no one better than herself, Josie, to confide in either. To say anything to a village girl and her secret would be all over the county. Whatever would she do?

'You haven't told Auntie Betty?'

'No!'

'Will he marry you?'

'He can't think about anything but going off to the army. I'm sure he doesn't want to get married – he's only seventeen, for heaven's sake – he'd think it barmy. How can I tell him?'

Josie had no answers for Maureen. There weren't any. They sat snivelling, brains whirling, egos at rock-bottom until, in the way of things, it seemed so stupid that they started giggling.

'Perhaps a bomb'll drop on us tomorrow and then nothing will matter.'

'Perhaps you're not really pregnant.'

'No, I'm not sure yet. But I think so.'

'Perhaps Auntie Betty will love having a baby. Why not?'

'You can imagine when I tell them! Dad'll go potty ... but what about you? Perhaps when Jumbo's got two legs, he'll never come back. Or he'll run away. And Chris is going, then you'll have no one.'

'Don't say that! Do you think I don't think it?'

Then Josie stopped giggling and flung herself down on the bed and wept.

'Oh don't!' Maureen wailed. 'I didn't mean it!'

'But it's true,' Josie sobbed.

Maureen started to cry again. They could no longer see a funny side to anything, so they undressed and got into bed. It was well into September and their little room, the window open, had a crisp evening smell of earth and apples from the tree outside, drooping now with fruit. Everything out there was just the same, Josie thought, and always would be: death and birth was all part of it, like the seasons, like rain, like sunshine, on and on. But nothing would ever be the same for her any more, not after loving Chris.

When Chris came out of the pub with Peter, he found Jumbo sitting on the wall, waiting for him. Chris by then had had more to drink than usual and Jumbo was coldly sober.

'Just a minute,' Jumbo said.

'Not now, for God's sake,' Chris said. 'I'm in no state.'

'It won't take long, what I want to say to you.'

Peter said softly to Chris, 'I'll wait in the car.'

Chris watched him go away across the car park with a sense of having been dropped down a deep, cold well. His head could have done with just that, but not his soul. He was alone with his brother.

'Josie told me you're taking her down to London for the night. I know how it is between you. I've guessed for a while. I'm not stupid. I'm used to it, after all. I just want to tell you that, this time, it's not like the other times. I wouldn't be sorry if tomorrow, when you fly out, you don't come back, that's all.'

'It's quite likely,' Chris said.

'I wanted you to know.'

'Thank you.'

'I've prayed for you every night. But no more.'

'OK. Understood.'

Chris couldn't bring himself to explain, to say sorry, to pull out. Only let the words take their sad place in his disordered brain. Jumbo got off the wall and reached for his crutches.

Chris said, 'We can give you a lift back, if you like.'

'Sod your lift.'

He swung away into the darkness. Chris went over to where Peter sat waiting in the MG.

'Not good?'

'No. Not good. Get home, I want to be unconscious.'

He got in the car and slammed the door. Peter started the engine.

'It'll be over for us soon. Just hold on, then we've got our leave. I thought Skye. What do you think?'

'Oh my God, Skye! Yes. Yes. I can face that.'

It swept over him with a force that shook his addled brain still further: the jagged peaks of the Cuillins, bruise purple in the Scottish clouds, an eagle hanging, the sea far, far below like a great sheet of glittering silver, not a sound save of the wind and distant gulls. He felt himself reaching out for it with a wrenching longing, panacea for his disordered mind. He was starved of peace.

'Yes, Pete. We can fly up. Wizard. I hadn't got as far as thinking what to do with a leave. Only that it would be with you.'

'I'll have to see the parents first, just a night. They'll understand I'll want Skye more than them. I've got the map somewhere in my gear. I'll fish it out when we get back.'

The little car bombed down the road. The air was cold and swept over Chris's fevered body with a calming breath. They went into the barracks and to the small bleak room they shared. Peter turned on the shaded blueish light between the beds and started rummaging in a drawer for the map of Skye. Chris sat on his bed, undoing his shoes, pulling off his tie.

Jumbo's white face seemed suddenly to be back in front of him.

I wouldn't be sorry if tomorrow you didn't come home. I've prayed for you every night. But no more.

Skye was suddenly very far away, a dream, no more. He put his face in his hands and started to cry.

Peter straightened up and came to him. He pulled back the blankets of the strictly made service bed.

'Here, get in, old chap. Sleep it off. It won't be so bad in the morning.'

Chris crumpled into the bed and buried his face in the pillow, still sobbing. Peter pulled the blankets back over him. He switched off the light, went to the window and pulled the blackout curtains aside.

A barn owl, ghostly white, was flying against the dark background of the woods. He watched it, biting his lip. The sky was clear, awash with stars. A fine night, another fine day tomorrow. No respite.

He could easily have wept too.

Chapter Twelve

The dogfight was very high, almost invisible. The sky was cloudless, patterned with scribbles of white, like a child's drawing, circles and wavering lines. The faint scream of over-taxed engines sounded more like bees in a garden than war. The country people looked up, shaded their eyes into the sun, then went on with their work. If it came low they would run into the shelter of trees and hedges.

A Hurricane was running for home with three 109s on its tail. Its pilot was praying that they were too close to their fuel limit to think of chasing him far, but guessed that enthusiasm – he a sitting duck! – would overcome their prudence. As it proved. There was a stunning explosion which blew his eardrums and the engine in front of him was suddenly a blinding mass of flame. And this, he knew: one clear, cold shred of his consciousness was reminding him that this was the scenario that all pilots dreaded so much that they never spoke of it, even in jest, even while his instinct was already in action for survival. The smell of burning flesh, his own, filled his sizzling nostrils with a disgusting stench while his disintegrating hand sought the release pin of his harness straps. Thank God the cockpit hood was already open. He rolled the machine over and fell out, a blazing torch, into the icy air.

If he fell far and fast enough would he put out the flames that devoured him? Bomber pilots were known to dive to the limit to put out an engine fire, he knew. The innate instinct for survival already had him groping to find the ripcord of his parachute. But his hands did not work. The flesh on them was dark and bubbling, the fingers like sausages frying.

'You bastard, you bastard – pull it! For God's sake!'

Was there a God? He had always thought so, until now. He forced the smoking hand to the ripcord and, after what seemed an eternity, was able to hook the ring and pull. What if the parachute was burned too? Did he want to live, after all? Why was he fighting so hard to continue a life that would be nothing but unbearable pain and horror? Yet as the great silk cloud of the parachute opened over him his last thought was of infinite relief.

The watchers below saw half a parachute open and the other half fly away in charred shreds. The body below stopped momentarily, swinging in hopeless arcs through the sky, and then started to fall again, faster and faster.

Too fast.

'Jesus Christ!' breathed one of the fieldhands.

Smoking, grilled, the body hurtled down, the parachute a broken string trailing. It hit the ground at sixty miles an hour.

The people watching could not move.

Chapter Thirteen

It was the longest day Josie could ever remember. She did not know how she was going to cope with Chris going away. The thought of the parting crucified her.

Yet he would be going out of danger for the time being. She knew everyone coped; they had to. There were other girls on the airfield in love with pilots, there were mothers like Mrs Patterson, wives everywhere with the same dread: of seeing the telegraph boy coming down the road on his bicycle, whistling, little pillbox hat perched awry, bringing the small buff envelope: 'I regret to inform you . . .' It was everyday stuff, not just her own stupid panic. And proper people would laugh at her: that a child could be in love as she was in love. Calf love, her mother called it sneeringly. But her mother had known! Auntie Betty's story had staggered Josie. She was going to tell her mother that she knew about it, and see if her iron mother would melt. Josie had never known the mother her aunt had described. But would she dare?

Anything could happen.

Chris had said he would come about seven, when they were stood down. She had her suitcase packed, and tried to dress as prettily as possible without arousing Auntie Betty's suspicions. She was only going home to her mother, so they thought. She was still scorched by Jumbo's anger. She tried to dismiss it, but the way she had turned his euphoria about his leg so suddenly into that terrible anger was a memory that would not leave her. Dear gentle Jumb . . . she had never guessed that he was capable of such bitter passion. But she could not bear to have her own joy suppressed. Now Chris had said he was being posted and they were going to be parted it mattered all the more, to take this last magical night together. Whatever Jumbo's reaction, she could not forego her own chance of happiness. She had never been together with Chris since that one strange day by the lake, only together in snippets of time, coming and going. Sometimes she thought she only meant anything to Chris because she was a sort of dream apart from his dreadful working day, etched into his mind by that first surreal meeting. He had been a bit concussed, she thought. But he had been sober enough since, and still professed to love her.

The evening started to close in with all the autumnal hints of darker times ahead. Uncle Bert came home, grumbling about the lack of light in the cowshed, Auntie Betty dished up baked beans and fried eggs and pulled the blackout curtains across.

'You'll be travelling in the dark at this rate. I reckon

it's not safe, those dimmed lights on the car. You make sure he goes slow.'

'That lad go slow?' Bert snorted. 'That'll be a first time.'

'Edna'll be waiting up for you. She'll be so thrilled to see you again.'

It was gone seven and Josie's mouth was dry. She had to eat her supper, every mouthful threatening to choke her. Maureen was out with Tom; the wireless played Harry Hall and his dance band. Josie pushed the beans round and round her plate.

'I'm not hungry.'

'You will be by the time you get to Wimbledon. I don't suppose Edna gets extra eggs like we do. You'll find a difference down there, my girl, away from the farm. Just the rations, no perks.'

Josie was straining her ears to hear the sound of the MG coming up the lane. She had not expected him to be late.

'You'd have done better to have gone on the train this morning. I said so all along.'

'It's cheaper, a free ride,' Bert said. 'If he comes, that is.'

Josie wanted to scream. She got up from the table. 'I think I can hear him.'

She went to the door.

'Mind the blackout!'

Josie went out with a sob of frustration. But there was a car coming up the lane. She stood there in the cold air and watched the little slitty lights jerking as the car fell into the ruts. An enormous rush of relief and elation flooded over her.

'Chris!' she called out. Then remembered that Auntie Betty must not see how she loved him. She made herself stand still. The car pulled up and Chris climbed out. Josie saw that he was in his best uniform, very smart, and it struck her that he was not her usual Chris, but almost a stranger. Was it just the uniform? He moved wearily and his face was strained and pale. He came round and put his arm round her shoulders and gave her a brief hug.

'Are you ready? Shall we go?'

'I'll get my case and say goodbye. I'm all ready, yes.'

'I'm sorry I'm late. Something – something happened. I had to stay a bit.'

'Are you all right?'

'Yes. Let's get going and I'll tell you.'

She fetched her things and her aunt and uncle came out to say goodbye.

'Why, you'll catch your death in that thing with no roof!' Auntie Betty said.

'I've got my greatcoat to put round her,' Chris said. 'I thought of it.'

'Well, that's something. Just drive carefully, for heaven's sake, now it's dark and you've no lights to speak of.'

'Yes, I will. I promise. I know the road very well. I'll look after her.'

Josie was away at last, shuddering down the lane. She buried her face in the greatcoat, smelling Chris in the thick wool, pulling it close. She knew there was something wrong.

'What is it?'

'Look, it doesn't make any difference to us tonight, what's happened. He wouldn't want it. But it's Peter. He was killed this morning.'

Josie gasped.

'But—'

'It was always going to happen, one of us.'

'We can't—!'

'We will. More so, because of it. What would you rather I do tonight? Lie on my bed sobbing? How would that help? I thought I wouldn't tell you, but I knew it wasn't possible. I need you tonight, Josie, more than ever. You'll see how it is when we get there, I need you. I don't want to be alone.'

Josie wasn't capable of words in the situation. Peter . . . it could so easily have been Chris, as Chris well knew. To brazen it out, shrug it off, not think . . . it was a way of dealing with it, a terrible way. The only way not to go under. How did she know? She had no idea.

And then he was talking of something else, to her astonishment. His voice was lighter, something about a car one of the pilots had bought and in the glove locker he had found a bundle of letters and when he read them . . . Josie could not follow. Her head was spinning. In spite of the lack of light the car was whizzing along. There was scarcely any other traffic on the road. She found it impossible to follow his conversation, and pulled the heavy coat round herself in shuddering silence.

Until Chris said, 'Snap out of it, Josie, else I'll dump you here on the road. Can't you see how it is for me?'

'Of course I can! That's why I—'

'If we're not going to enjoy ourselves there's no point going.'

'Yes, OK. What if we hadn't made this date then? What would you have done?'

'God knows. I'm just eternally grateful we've got it. It puts it off.'

What it put off Josie didn't like to ask. Grieving? Shooting oneself? Just living? If he could put it out of his mind so could she. She scarcely knew Peter, after all, although she had always been aware of the strength of his presence. Had Chris seen him shot down? They were going on leave together. She pulled herself together.

'Where are we going?' she asked. 'I've never been to a nightclub.'

'No? Well, you'll see. It's just drinking and dancing, lots of noise. And we'll eat. Champagne and all. You'll like it, Josie, I promise. You can forget everything when you're in there, all together, all in the same boat. Loving, parting, going mad together. You'll see.'

'Better than Albert's?'

He laughed.

'Albert does his best. We've had some good nights there. You like my car, eh? One of my riggers souped it up for me. It can get a real move on now. Listen to it!'

He started to laugh, putting his foot down. It was glorious – shades of Sidney's Red Hunter . . . how long ago that seemed! If Chris could turn his mind from death, she had no alternative but to go with him, unpractised as she was. Her brain was already scrambled: just scramble it some more. Going to a party when it should have been a funeral – what was the difference? Both celebrations of a kind, of life, of death.

London was not so far away in an MG, for quite soon the fields began to give way to factories and suburbs. Although it was dark, they were lucky to be travelling with a full moon in the sky.

'I know my way to the West End but God knows how we're going to find Wimbledon. Out by Knightsbridge, I think. I hope your mother's not waiting up.'

'I know the way!' She had been once or twice with Sidney on the motorbike. How long ago that seemed now! 'My mother doesn't matter!'

Nothing mattered any more, Josie decided. Chris was laughing. And eventually the interminable suburbs gave way to the heavy Victorian edifices of the City and the grace of the Georgian squares where the great old plane trees were just starting to lose their summer green. In Holborn, although no lights showed, there were plenty of people still about, mostly men in uniform with girls on their arms gathering outside the theatres and cinemas or businessmen in bowler hats and office girls on their way home after working late. Josie had almost forgotten urban life, steeped in the farming somnolence of her adopted home, and felt her spirits warm to the strident voices and laughter that echoed from the pavements. London's night life seemed as healthy as ever. The darkness was strange but the smells and sounds were familiar, wrapping round her. The gaunt façade of the National Gallery was so dear, the lions still watching out from the square, the fountains still – where were the great paintings now? 'Stored in some Welsh slate mines,' Chris said, 'or so I read somewhere.'

'Poor things! So far from home.'

'Very far from home, most of them. Snitched from Italy and Greece and all over by rolling rich British aristocrats. My great-grandfather bought a Rembrandt for fifty quid in Amsterdam, can you believe? But my stupid grandmother sold it when he died. Think how rich we'd be now!'

'How wonderful, to own a great painting! Fancy selling it! I would love to own a real painting, have one for my own.'

'My ma's got some nice ones, but all of horses. Rather boring.'

They drove down Piccadilly and turned right somewhere: a large square, then some narrow streets, a small square, more a garden, dark doorways facing, the faint sound of dance music. Chris parked the car.

'This is a good place. You can eat, and then they've got a dance floor downstairs. You'll like it.'

Josie had never been to such a place in her life. It

seemed sophisticated beyond belief; she felt about five years old, even in her best dress and wearing lipstick and Maureen's gold sandals. It was well lit inside the curtained doors, with a huge, crowded bar and little tables set for dinner, mostly just for two, awash with laughter and loud conversation, the air thick with cigarette smoke. It was full of servicemen and their girls, mainly RAF men, and quite a lot of the girls were WAAFs. Josie noticed immediately that Chris commanded considerable attention from the women, eyes flicking from his looks to his officer's insignia, pilot's wings and DFC ribbon, and she marvelled that he had chosen her for a partner when he could have had anyone. She remembered only too clearly what Jumbo had said about girls falling out of the trees for him. Just as she had. Oh Jumbo, forgive me, I can't help it! she almost cried out then, and Chris hugged her close, following a waiter who beckoned them to a table in a little alcove.

'It's nice to see you again, sir,' the waiter said.

He brought the wine list and the menu and gave Josie smooth, practised attention, in spite of the fact that she knew he was thinking: Cor blimey, what's he brought in tonight?

'And what will madam have to drink?'

She panicked, looking to Chris for advice. It clearly wasn't a ginger beer sort of place.

'We'll have champagne,' Chris said. 'It's special tonight.'

The menu was brief and expensive.

'What's money?' said Chris.

'You order. I like anything.'

An officer in uniform came up and shouted, 'Chris Patterson, you old trout! Haven't seen you since Vassincourt! How's things?'

Then someone else: 'Crikey, it's old Chris! Where've you been, matey?'

A very elegant WAAF officer: 'Why, Chris darling, how lovely to see you!' Raking eyes over Josie, who blushed crimson.

Chris said to her, 'I'm sorry about this. We should have gone somewhere else, I didn't think.'

But Josie was excited by the atmosphere and impressed by Chris's circle of friends. She felt she was high in a completely alien social world, looking at herself blushing and fumbling over the knives and forks. Chris was at home, amongst his kind. She wasn't his kind, she knew. What was he thinking of, taking her?

'Chris! Great to see you! It's been a long time! God, that night in Neuville with Peter and Bossy – do you remember? That must be the last time I set eyes on you, all of us in the back of that cart going home, and then when we got back those devils strafing us – what a night, eh? How is Pete, by the way, still with you?'

'Yeah, fine. He's fine.'

Chris's face went taut, blank. The man passed on. Josie shivered. Chris picked up his champagne glass and raised it.

'Here's to Peter,' he said softly.

Josie held hers out and they clinked together. She felt a dreadul lump come up in her throat, seeing the expression on Chris's face.

But then he laughed.

'We live with it, dying,' he said. 'It's amazing.'

Then in a second he was talking about his car and the trouble he'd had with its suspension. 'Lucky we've got all those mechanics on the ground. Not that they get much time for anything other than beat-up aeroplanes, but if you let them borrow your car when they've got it up and running – they're great. Motorbikes too – they can fix anything.'

'I like motorbikes. I used to go on one, down the bypass. It's smashing.'

'Jumbo and I – we had one. Well, that was a disaster, as you know. It was my fault, he was riding pillion. I lost control and we went through a hedge and down a bank. The bike landed on him, that's what did for his leg. And I didn't have a scratch on me. It was terrible – it should have been me, my fault and all. But he's never said a word of blame, not ever. But it's something I have to carry with me, the blame. And now this. I'm a bastard, Josie. I can't help it. What I did to Jumbo and now this, again – with you, when you're his girl. I hate myself, I can't tell you.'

'I feel bad about Jumbo too,' Josie whispered, shattered by Chris's revelations.

Chris reached for the bottle of champagne and refilled their glasses.

'It helps to drink. Forget. It's what it's for. But tonight, Josie, we'll not think of all these things, else we might as well have stayed at home. Things work out, in the end.'

'Yes. All right.'

Already she knew the drink was taking her, unpractised as she was. The food was delicious, but she could hardly have said what it was. She could not take her eyes off Chris, watching his fleeting expressions, seeing his grief covered, a nervous tic at the corner of one eye. To be with him, she wanted it to last for ever. But she was on her way home, to exchange his company for her mother's.

When the meal was over he led her downstairs into a smoky-dark dance hall, where an orchestra was playing the current, nostalgic hits of the day that centred on exactly their situation: farewells and uncertainties and memories of carefree times. To the dreamy beat couples revolved with their arms wrapped round each other, heads on shoulders, eyes shut. Chris took Josie in his arms and held her close, and she put her face against him with a sigh and felt herself melt away – or so it seemed – totally, gloriously as one with him, the sentimental music washing over her like a blessing. It had never been like this in ballroom dancing lessons at school; is this what they had been preparing her for? She doubted it. This bliss beyond knowing: loving, warm, moving in rhythm together, loving, loving . . . He put his head down and kissed the back of her neck and her ears and her temple. 'My dear little Josie. I shall never forget you in that wood, and when I woke up you were still there. I thought I had died and was in paradise. Your face, amongst the leaves, all eyes, like a little deer. My Josie.'

'I couldn't leave you. I never want to leave you, not ever. Never, never.'

'In my heart I shall never leave you.'

'But in yourself you will. Tonight.'

'That's how it is, Josie. It is for everyone, not just us. It's the way of the world.'

'I can't bear it!'

'You will, you will.'

And then the music grew faster and cheerful and they did not want it any longer, just standing with their arms round each other, kissing, and Chris said, 'We don't want to be here any longer. Let's go somewhere quiet,' and they went up the stairs and out to the car. Chris drove away, out to Piccadilly and away through Knightsbridge towards the Portsmouth Road.

'To Wimbledon, to deliver you to your mother. We are late, she will be angry. We can't part like this, Josie, outside your door with your mother being angry.'

'No, we can't. Stop on the common and we will say goodbye and then I'll walk home. I shall think about you all the way. And you can drive back, and think about me all the way.'

'Yes, that's best.'

The common where she had lain with Sidney: it had not changed. Somehow Chris was driving the little car over the hummocky grass, through the bracken and the birch trees and into a glade. The moon shone down through the leaves and nothing moved. When the engine died it was quite silent, as if they were at home by the lake. Josie turned to Chris and he took her in his arms and wrapped her round and hugged her, then he lifted her out and carried her across the soft turf and laid her on the grass and lay with her, close and warm. It was all she wanted, had ever wanted, she thought, not like with Sidney.

'I love you so!' she whispered.

It was hopeless, she knew it: nothing was in their favour, save the moon and the sweet-smelling grass and their own ardour. One did not arrange such things: it happened, sweet and fierce and incredible, way out of her experience, beyond imagining. She saw the stars spinning, the moonlight shining in Chris's eyes; she was laughing, crying, emotions fragmented, shattered. Nothing made sense: the bliss of their love and the searing grief of parting mixed incoherently, hopelessly.

She clung to him. 'Oh, Chris, I can't bear for you to go back. I can't bear it!'

He covered her face with kisses, licked up her tears, held her gently in his arms.

'It's all over for us, Josie,' he whispered. 'It's all over.'

He drove away over the common and stopped the car where she told him, at the top of the hill.

'I want to walk the rest. I need to.'

She got out, grabbing her old suitcase. It was terrible seeing him for the last time, silent, looking up at her. He had to be back at the airfield at dawn, she knew, and already she felt the darkness draining, heard the first bird call from the plane trees down the hill. She ran. The street was deserted and her footsteps echoed from the shop fronts. She heard the car reverse behind her, turn and drive away, the noisy engine fading into the distance. She went on running, crying and gasping until a stitch gripped her side and she stopped. She was halfway down the hill on familiar ground, as if she had never been away, save it was two o'clock in the morning and her heart was wrenched out of her: she was moving out of mere habit, brain unconnected. It was not the champagne that was unhinging her, only love. Love! It happened to everybody, she remembered, even to dumb Maureen, to her mother. It was nothing special.

Then she realized that it was cold, and Maureen's sandals were not for walking in. She sat down on the pavement and unpacked her ordinary shoes and exchanged them, locked up her suitcase again and walked on. Nothing seemed real any more. She passed a few people, a man on a bicycle labouring up, a young couple laughing, down past the school and the shops and into Worple Road. Too early for the trolley buses whose wires hung silently against the sky, too early for the birds, too late for her mother. She was tired now beyond caring, her brain gone dead with exhaustion. She ached all over. Coming up to her road she thought to comb her hair and brush her coat down and wipe her face over with her handkerchief.

Whatever must she look like? What on earth was she going to say, arriving home in the small hours?

Her mother had waited up, of course.

She opened her door at Josie's knock.

'Whatever time do you call this?' she asked angrily. And then, quite unexpectedly, she said chokingly, 'Josie! Josie! How I've missed you!' and put her arms round Josie, hugging her close. 'Oh Josie, my dear, I'm so glad to have you back!'

'Mum, I've missed you too. It seems ages—'

'Your father's not here. It's his night for fire-watching at the office. Come along, sit down, and I'll make a cup of tea before we go to bed. Why are you so late? Who is this fellow that brought you? Betty just said a friend. I've been so worried. What happened?'

Josie did the best she could on the spur of the moment. 'He's from the airfield. We were late starting and then we broke down. He couldn't help it, and there was no way of letting you know. He had to go to London on business so it seemed to make sense, bringing me.'

'Oh well, you're here now, that's what matters. I haven't got to go in tomorrow. I thought I couldn't just go off to work on your first day so I wangled some leave. Why, how grown-up you seem! I hardly know you now!'

In the shaded light of the kitchen they both tried to sum each other up, slightly embarrassed after the first outburst. Josie thought her mother had changed too,

170

looking about ten years younger, the cross frowning lines smoothed from her face. It must be working, going out, meeting people, having a purpose in life that had wrought the change, Josie supposed. Her mother had always been bad-tempered, perhaps just with boredom. Now, just when Josie wanted to weep, her mother was all smiles.

'Country life must suit you – you look so well! I thought you would die of it, staying with Betty . . .'

Her mother, who used to talk little, now couldn't stop. Josie let it wash over her until: 'Why, I do believe you're falling asleep! Come on, up to bed. You can tell me all about it in the morning.'

If only! Josie groped her way up the stairs.

'Your tea, sir. Four o'clock. Are you awake, sir?'

Chris thought he hadn't slept, but he was wrong. Heavily, heavily asleep, he stirred irritably at his batman's insistence.

'Yes, yes, go away.'

He rolled over, opened his eyes.

'I'm OK. Yes.'

It was still dark save for the shaded lamp beside his bed. The blackout curtains were drawn and the room was cold and empty. Chris remembered immediately that he was the only one their batman had to wake; there were to be no answering snuffles and groans from Peter. Not ever. Just silence.

Well, they had known. It was no surprise. One or other of them, or both. If it had been himself, his

171

troubles would be over. Jumbo . . . there was no way he could face Jumbo again. Face the sky without Peter? He had no choice. He lay on his back looking at the cracks in the ceiling, cold and sick.

Across the room Peter's effects – photographs, letters, binoculars, civvy clothes and knick-knacks – were laid out on his bed waiting to be docketed and sent home. Chris's job. His best things – fur-lined boots, his motorbike, his golf-clubs – had already been appropriated, as was the way of things. The empty bed was the worst thing of all, the worst that had happened so far. If Peter had been there, his inner turmoil might have been soothed. The ghastly scene with Jumbo. Peter had that way. On top of the effects was the map of Scotland, still opened at Skye, where they had been planning to go on Saturday. Chris got up and folded it shut and threw it in the waste-bin. He went to the washbasin and started to shave. His hand was trembling. He had noticed this lately. He couldn't see what he was doing and cut himself. He swore. He tried not to think about last night. What he had done was unforgivable. He put the thought away, closed it shut like the map of Skye. Today he would take Peter's place leading the squadron. Soon it would be light and there was work to do.

He was very tired. The trite saying 'tired to death' came to his mind, fitting his feeling exactly. He sat down on his own bed and stared at Peter's, so neatly made up with clean sheets for the next comer, so neat, so perfect. Everything about Peter was neat and

172

perfect: his reliability, his kindness, strength, courage, intelligence, humour. His simplicity, love for birds, fishing, a country pub. They had become dangerously close, thrown together in the act of war, choosing to be together on leave, in spite of family and girls, a friendship bound by the closeness of death. It had come now, as lately they had known it would. He did not know if he could go on without Peter.

But there was no alternative.

He got up and forced himself to face the day. Go to the mess to see if there was any coffee. Because of Peter it would be grim this morning. He knew only too well the looks on people's faces, especially towards someone whose best mate had gone. He had to do it. The new day was breaking. It just went on. There was no way out.

Chapter Fourteen

Josie was woken by the sun flooding across her pillow. Her bedroom at Auntie Betty's had faced north. The sun on her pillow told her she was home, almost before her eyes opened. The how and the why of it came more slowly, filling her with hopelessness. To be back at Auntie Betty's now was all she wanted, to see Chris's plane go out, to meet him when he came back. Just to see him. Oh to see him! How could she get through the day, pretending to her mother that life was just the same as when she had left?

But her mother was so cheerful, bringing her a cup of tea, sitting on the bed, chatting away. Josie's silence wasn't noticed. Her mother was a new person now she had a job and a purpose in life.

'Now you're coming back to go to the art school we can carry on quite easily, out all day, and I'll be back in time to make tea for you and Daddy. You'll have to go up there and find out when term starts – it's quite soon, I think. Everything's at sixes and sevens and perhaps they've no idea how many pupils will be starting.'

'I'm not going back to Auntie Betty's?'

'Just to get your things and say goodbye, perhaps. If the bombs are dropping up there on that airfield you're just as safe down here. It's a complete lottery where the bombs fall, so it really doesn't matter where you are. We've all got used to it now. When the sirens go I don't bother to go in the shelter any more, only if they're overhead. We're not a target here, but when the bombers are scattered or lost they just drop their load anywhere. You might just as well get on with your life.'

Josie found it hard to believe this was happening. Somehow she had completely put out of her mind that she wasn't just here for a visit, that she was taking up her old life and ambition: to go to the art school. Her surroundings were totally familiar, yet she felt she was not really any part of it. She didn't belong anywhere any more. Only with Chris, which wasn't possible.

'We'll have some breakfast and then do a bit of shopping. I've got an appointment at the hairdresser's, and you can have a look round while you're waiting. You must be starved of shops out in that countryside. How Betty endures it I've never fathomed, when she was brought up in a perfectly nice place. I felt really sorry for you exiled up there but when we sent you we didn't know how things were going to turn out. It's different now. We've stopped them in their tracks now, they say, thanks to our fighter boys . . .'

She was rabbiting on but Josie hardly heard her. Her mother – her new, all-conquering mother – did not notice her silences, such was her own torrent of talk about this and that. Josie supposed she had something to talk about now, when before she had just stayed in the house all day trying to think of something to do besides housework and knitting.

'It'll be nice for you to see some shops. If you've got some coupons left we can get you something new – you look as if you can do with some new shoes, and a skirt perhaps, to start at the art school.'

Josie decided to see how many of her old friends were still around after she got back from the shopping round with her mother. She would go up to Mary's: she must be back by now to start school again . . . she could go back and see Matty. Then she thought, Not yet; it wasn't possible to talk about anything sanely, not after last night. Perhaps Jumbo, in Richmond . . . but how could she face Jumbo after she had betrayed him?

'You're very quiet,' her mother said. 'Are you feeling well?'

'Yes, I'm all right.'

'Let's go then. Get your cardigan. We'll walk down.'

She had forgotten how her mother loved shopping, trying things on: hats especially. She had forgotten about trailing round behind her in the department stores, in Marshall and Snelgrove, Bourne and Hollingsworth, Liberty, trying on hats and dresses, eyeing shoes, exclaiming over ball gowns, fingering rolls of fabric. She didn't go up to London for shopping now because of the danger: Ely's in Wimbledon or

Bentalls in Kingston-on-Thames had to do. But the examination of goods was just as intensive. Josie trailed along in a dream, nodding agreement to the remarks, seeing nothing. When her mother left her to go to the hairdressing department she went for a coffee, not even raising the enthusiasm to spend the time in the bookshop up the road where she had browsed for hours in the past. She sat there thinking of Chris, reliving every minute of the evening before, feeling him, smelling him, his smoky breath, his cold cheek, the feel of his floppy hair through her fingers, the smell of air force soap and the hint of oil, of aeroplane, of his warm body holding her to the sad strains of 'We'll Meet Again' on the dance floor. 'Don't know where, don't know when' were the next prophetic words that hung in the thick blue air of the crowded dance hall – how true and apt the words of the sentimental song. Josie wondered how on earth she was going to get back to Auntie Betty's in the near future to see Chris again.

She had scarcely moved from her abstraction over the coffee cup before her mother came to collect her, her hair in smart waves and curls.

'It really sets you up, to look nice. It's hard to find time to get to a hairdresser's these days.'

She had never bothered before. It was amazing how she had changed.

'But you're very quiet, Josie, not the girl I remembered. Is this what country living has done for you? You haven't argued with me once.'

Josie tried to laugh.

'Is it someone you're missing?'

How sharp she was, her nose questing like a dog's.

'No, no! I – I—' She floundered.

At that opportune moment the awful wail of an air-raid warning siren echoed through the busy store. Josie had never heard one so close before and it made her jump. The shoppers started to drift downstairs, but not with any urgency.

'Oh damn it,' said her mother. 'We'd better go home. You never know how long these things are going to last.'

She gathered her things together and drank down her coffee.

'Come along.'

They went out of the shop and into the street. Distant thumps of anti-aircraft fire could be heard and the faint, familiar whine of fighters very high up. People were queuing up to get on the bus as usual and there was no sign of panic. But her mother walked more quickly than usual.

As they got near home, the high, distant throb of a bomber came from the south and the anti-aircraft fire from the common opened up. Josie looked up and saw a single Heinkel quite clearly. Black anti-aircraft fire started to blossom around it.

'Let's get inside – the shrapnel from the guns is worse than the bombs,' her mother said, opening the garden gate. She was fumbling for her key.

Josie looked up and actually saw the first bombs

falling from the Heinkel. The whistle of their falling crescendoed through the air. She fell through the front door, pushed by her mother.

'Under the stairs! Under the stairs, quick!'

There was no time to run for the shelter in the garden. The first bomb landed with a distant crump as Josie fell into the dark cupboard amongst the brooms, mops, buckets and vacuum cleaner.

'Get in, get in! Oh, how I hate this!' her mother moaned. 'The bastards, the bastards!'

Her mother swearing! Josie crouched down, and heard the next whistle clearly descending. There was an enormous explosion which lifted her off her feet, blasting her eardrums, crashing her head against the roof of the cupboard, then a terrible rumble of falling masonry and everything went black. She screamed, but could not hear her own voice for the reverberations in her head, like the thunder of surf, crashing, vibrating her brain-box. Everything was black. She did not know whether her eyes were open or shut, what was up and what was down. The noise in her head crucified her. She did not move, or could not – she didn't know which – but she wasn't hurt, could feel no pain, could breathe, but was petrified all the same, not sure whether she was alive or dead. What was dead like? Perhaps this was dead?

But no. Perhaps she had been unconscious for a while but slowly, slowly, painfully, she knew she was alive. She was breathing, although the air choked her with dust. She could move: there was space around her. But it was black, totally black, eyes shut or open. There was a whimpering noise (herself), various slitherings and creakings and thumpings as of a bombed house settling, no human voices, no screams, no more bombs.

'Mum?'

Silence.

But her mother had been, must still be, there . . .

'Mum!'

Josie felt the panic rising. Her mother had been right beside her. She put out her hand and touched something soft. Flesh. Something hard. Wood. She herself, she now realized, was lying on the floor of the cupboard, no doubt flung down by the blast, but there was nothing pinning her down. She could move all her body, but the space she was in was tiny. All this realization came slowly, by feel. She could only lift her head a foot or so before it came up against something hard. The flesh she was touching was her mother's arm.

'Mum!'

She shook the arm but no answer came. She groped up the limb and started to feel towards her mother's heart. She laid her palm over her mother's breast and felt the heart beating steadily beneath it. The flood of relief made her start crying. Her mother was unconscious but alive. More exploration found that the staircase had caved in and the timber was lying across her mother's lower body, pinning her down. Josie tried to lift it but it was impossible, weighed down from above by what was probably bricks and mortar. It did not move an inch. Whether her mother was injured underneath it she could not tell.

'Mum, oh Mum! Speak to me! Are you all right?'

She felt for her mother's face, brushing the dust away, and found her eyelids closed, her lips slightly parted, no signs of injury. Her breath came softly, evenly. Her smart waves and curls were full of dust and plaster. Surely if she was injured she would not be breathing so easily? Josie's hot tears mingled with the dirt.

'Mum, wake up, wake up! Are you all right?'

She still could not see anything at all, as if she were blindfolded. No pinpricks of the bright sunshine outside found their way through the masonry that covered them. Oh God, they might suffocate! Were there people out there going to rescue them? There must be! But usually the house was empty at this time of day . . . panicky thoughts whirled round her brain.

'Mum, oh come on, wake up!'

She lay close to her mother, willing her to recover consciousness. Suppose she never did! But she tried to keep cool. Keep cool like Chris. And Peter. Facing death, not panicking. Keep cool. It was only a small semi lying on top of them, not Blenheim Palace. She was safe now in her little black tomb, not facing machine-gun fire . . . it was only a matter of waiting. Not to panic! Not to use up the air: breathe slowly, softly. Be brave. Be like Chris. Oh Chris! Lie beside me again, Chris. I love you so!

She stifled these thoughts that made her sob. She tore her brain away to cool, boring things. She stroked her mother's face. She had always thought she did not love her mother, that she was an unnatural daughter, but now she thought she did. And her father, coming home tonight . . . what on earth would he feel, seeing his house bombed and no wife waiting with his tea? Josie scarely knew her father, so undemanding was his presence, so apart from her life. He spoke so little and hardly ever to her. Yet now she thought of him with great pangs of affection: Daddy, Daddy! I need you, come and rescue us! Oh Daddy!

'Josie!' her mother whispered. There was panic in her voice.

'I'm here, I'm here! I'm all right! Oh, Mum, and you – are you . . . ?'

Her mother groaned, tried to move, couldn't, groaned, wept. Josie stroked her face, whispering reassurance. But how did she know what was happening under the timber across her mother's legs? She might be bleeding to death.

'My legs, my legs, I can't move . . .'

'Lie still. Someone will come. We're not dead. Lie still, don't hurt yourself any more.'

Gradually her mother became aware of what had happened and she became calm and practical.

'You're all right – how lucky! We can't do anything save wait now. How lucky we're still alive!'

'Will they come?'

'Yes, yes, they always dig people out. They've had lots of practice. We'll have to shout to let them know we're here.'

'They might not hear.'

'No, but that's the drill. They listen.'

After a little while she said, 'You came back to keep away from the bombs over the airfield, remember? What a farce! Just look at you now! Betty will have a fit when she hears.'

'They say it has your number on it, wherever you are.'

'Yes, I believe in that.'

It was very strange, lying helpless in the dark, squashed close. Josie knew she had never been close to her mother but now she was, both literally and figuratively. Their minds were suddenly in total accord, focused. Lying there, she wondered if her mother was thinking the same: how the world could change in a second. They were entombed, shocked. She realized now that she felt very cold and was shivering. The dust in her throat was choking. She kept telling herself that she wasn't hurt, yet she found it hard to speak any more. She was shaking. She tried to stay calm, holding onto herself.

'My poor little girl,' her mother said. 'What a shock for you.'

'And my poor old mother, a shock for you too.' She tried to joke.

'We must be patient. They will come.'

'What about your legs? Do they hurt?'

'I can't feel anything, no. Can't move. I'm cold, that's all.'

'Yes, I've got the shivers.'

They huddled together.

'Perhaps we should shout,' her mother said.

So they took it in turns to shout. They didn't know what to shout. 'Help' seemed obvious, or just screaming, which was easier but felt cowardly.

'A whistle would be the thing.' But they didn't have a whistle.

'That'll do for a bit.'

The silence was as profound as the darkness. They lay there together, shivering. Then her mother said, 'Did you meet anyone up there? A boy, I mean?'

'Why do you ask?'

'You've changed.'

Josie hesitated to answer. Yes, she had changed. Was it so obvious? But, according to Auntie Betty, once love had changed her mother.

'Yes, I love someone.'

'I guessed. A country lad, a friend of Maureen's?'

'He's a pilot, a fighter pilot.'

'Oh my word! That's very unwise. Does he love you?'

'Yes, he does.'

'Oh Josie! How stupid!'

Josie was needled by her mother's remark, although sensing it was, perhaps, sympathetic rather than scornful.

'Auntie Betty told me about you, about your – your Freddie. And that he was killed.'

Her mother did not reply and there was a long silence. Josie regretted speaking out for they were in no situation to have one of their renowned arguments.

But then her mother gave a heavy sigh and said, 'Yes, dear Freddie. And that's why I wouldn't wish it on you, Josie, to love someone in such danger. I never think of it now, it's so long ago. But I remember how I suffered, far more than he did, getting killed. I shall never forget it. I try never to think about it, it was so awful. For years. I never met anyone else, you see, like most other girls seemed to. Some of them went through two or three great loves during the war.'

'How could they?!'

'Oh, in times of great uncertainty you take what happiness you can. But I never found anyone else.'

'What about Daddy?'

'That was much later. He was kind and good and I knew I would be stupid to pass up the chance of marriage. But he wasn't Freddie.'

'You've been happy together!'

'Yes, it worked out, don't get me wrong. He's been a good husband. I have no regrets. But there are things you never forget, even when you try to – how life can hurt. And now it seems you've put yourself in that situation.'

It was true, Josie knew.

Her mother said, 'But you're only young. Calf love, they call it.'

'But you were young too!'

'Yes. I was seventeen, eighteen.'

If there could be a stronger love than she felt for Chris (and, perhaps, than he felt for her), Josie could not imagine it. If it was slighted by elders, it was through jealousy. She could not talk about it but her mother did not pry. All she said was, 'When we get out of here, perhaps I will meet him. It looks as if you will have to go back to Betty's until we find somewhere else to live.'

'Oh, yes, I want to go back!'

The art school, her Mecca, could not compete with her love for Chris. But other couples parted, worked, still loved. She knew that. She would have to learn. Chris was going on leave anyway, and then he said he was to be posted. Squadrons which had a hard time were posted to somewhere quieter for their pilots to recover, she knew that.

'Just to see Chris before he goes away, then I will go to the art school.'

'We won't have anywhere to live!'

'You can come up to Auntie Betty's.'

'You must be joking! I've got my job in Kingston. I've got to go in tomorrow – they only gave me a couple of days off to see you. I couldn't live with Betty – we used to fight like wild cats. Oh my God, what shall I do?'

She started to cry.

'Oh, Mum, don't cry – it will be all right, honest it will.'

But after they had lain there for a long time without

hearing anything she began to wonder. They shouted and screamed at intervals, but lost all sense of time. The silence that hemmed them in, and the total darkness, was grimly oppressive and they started to recite all the poetry they could remember to keep their spirits up. Josie had learned huge chunks of Wordsworth, Keats and Shelley and miles of Shakespeare at school and, amazingly, it all came back quite easily, while her mother knew Christina Rossetti and Blake and 'The boy stood on the burning deck, Whence all but he had fled.'

'Then what? Everyone knows that.'

'The flame that lit the battle's wreck, Shone round him o'er the dead.'

'What battle was that?'

'I don't know.

'When I am dead, my dearest,
Sing no sad songs for me;
Plant thou no roses at my head,
Nor shady cypress tree.
Be the green grass above me
With showers and dew-drops wet;
And if thou wilt, remember,
And if thou wilt, forget.'

'Golly,' said Josie.

This was a mother she didn't know. Was her mother thinking they were going to die?

To cheer her up she quoted:
'The chief defect of Henry King
Was chewing little bits of string.
At last he swallowed some which tied
Itself in ugly knots inside.
Physicians of the utmost fame
Were called at once; but when they came
They answered; as they took their fees
"There is no cure for this disease."

'Listen! I heard something!'

They listened anxiously: a tinkling, rolling sort of noise, like dirt shifting, came from far away.

'Let's shout!'

They screamed and shouted madly, and thought they heard a reply. Or maybe it was wishful thinking. But then a distant knock.

'Oh thank God, I think they've come!'

It took ages, but the sounds came more and more clearly, and then muffled shouts. They shouted back.

'After all, it's a whole house they're moving,' Josie's mother said. 'And they have to be careful that nothing shifts and falls on us.'

She said her legs hurt. Her shivering got worse. Josie hugged her as best she could, thinking even as she did so how amazing it was, this closeness to her mother. But at least there was to be an end to it soon. What happened after that she had no idea. But with no house to live in, surely she had to go back to Auntie Betty's? She shivered now with excitement at the thought of seeing Chris again. Her heart was surging with her love, and her memories of saying goodbye last night were obliterated. He surely never meant it? It was impossible, when everything was coming right? Was she getting light-headed? The air was stifling. Did people die of suffocation under bomb rubble? She guessed they did.

More shouts and crashes from above. They shouted back. But it went on for ever, like rats scrabbling, then silence, then shouts and a crash. She called out, to give them a direction, and she heard a voice, 'We're coming, darling! Just hold on!' Something moved and a small shaft of light suddenly broke through. It was magical, like a sign from heaven. They both cried out with relief and excitement, and now nothing mattered but the increasing shifting and scraping going on above them and the further chinks that started to flitter here and there. They could hear the men's voices: 'Easy with this, mate,' and 'Steady on! You'll have the whole lot down,' and 'Get the crowbar under this, easy like.' It was all quite delicate, not to let anything heavy fall into their little cave, but after what seemed an incredibly long time the roof above them was lifted away and they were face to face with their rescuers. The grimy faces beamed with equal delight at the meeting.

'How are you, my ducks? All in one piece, eh? Cor, what luck!'

They pulled Josie out onto the huge pile of rubble which had once been her house. An ambulance stood in the street and a crowd of people stood around – gawping in the afternoon sunshine. Only their one house lay in ruins; the others on either side were still standing.

'Just the two of you in there, darling? Nobody else?'

'No, just me and my mother.'

The men greeted her like one of their own: she could see how comforting it was for them to be delivering unhurt people instead of mangled bodies. Their relief was as great as their own. What a job, she thought fleetingly! Her anxiety was for what lay under the beams across her mother's legs. But when they lifted her out and placed her on a stretcher Josie could see that the damage wasn't serious, more to her best stockings than anything else. But the men insisted on their going to hospital in the ambulance.

Her mother then started to weep and say, 'Whatever is Daddy going to do?' and in spite of kind re-assurances Josie then felt very shaky and weird and tearful, in spite of the amazing fact that they had survived an almost direct hit.

'It's shock, dear. You'll be fine after a good night's sleep,' the ambulance man said.

Would she? She wanted Chris, not a good night's sleep. Oh Chris! I nearly died, like you every day. I want you, I want you . . .

Chapter Fifteen

As always, even now, action banished the horrors of introspection, and as Chris took off at sunrise he felt that Peter was with him in the cockpit. It was a weird, not unhappy, feeling. They were so close in everything, it didn't seem as if death had made any difference: he was in Peter's place; Peter was with him. Chris was not afraid of command, knew it was coming to him shortly whether Peter was killed or not, and this morning he was sharing it with Peter. He spoke to him, could see him smiling. Rather see him than Josie. Last night, being with her, had saved him, but what it had done to her he didn't like to think. He didn't think.

It occurred to him that he was slightly light-headed. He had had scarcely three hours' sleep, and nine men depended on him to get it right. The RT was quiet, having given their initial course, no excitement. They climbed steadily and he was glad of the unusual somnolence of command, giving him time to settle in his unaccustomed position and calm his mind. No more sentiment, just a mind on the job. It wasn't difficult, given the beauty of the morning, the gorgeous panorama of sea and sky and curving earth surrounding him. It was incredible that this should be the arena they fought in, the sublime canopy mocking their stupid flylike activity in doing each other to death. The great ball of the sun over a glittering, calm sea looked too heavy to climb, suspended in the sky like a theatrical prop. It wasn't high enough to blind them yet, merely sending long shadows across the fields, drawing patterns on the ground, shafting through the cockpit cover. But it was the sky he should be looking into, searching, searching as always, not to be taken unawares, climbing steadily. It was routine now, but the beauty of being in the sky never failed to move him.

At least they had time to gain enough height before they met the first attackers. Chris saw them before the warning came and alerted the flight into battle, the familiar surge of adrenalin taking charge. This time there was Peter to avenge, and Chris screamed down head to head on the leading bomber, guns blazing, and was almost blown out of the sky by the ensuing explosion. Idiotic . . . he didn't care any more, aware now that he had damaged his own plane. Its steering was now all to hell, making him a sitting duck for the fighters that were tearing out of the sky like avenging locusts. The tracer flashed past and his fragile craft shuddered. It wouldn't make a climbing turn, only hang away like a wounded bird, so all he could do was let it go and wait for the finishing burst from behind. A fine way to end his first flight as leader was all that came into his mind, no panic, no fear. But his pursuer was now in trouble from Chris's number two, bringing deliverance, and after they had spun away in a private battle of their own Chris found himself alone, the battle raging far behind him. He could not return to it. The Hurricane would answer in its own good time, like a winged eagle, but the edge was gone. His bird was winged and needed all his help to bring it home.

Strange how often the heat of battle changed to peace and solitude within mere seconds. Chris was not unused to the situation. But this time there was no comfort, no relief as there usually was, only the great missing ache where Peter should have been, the anguish at what he had done to Josie and, most of all, Jumbo's words ringing in his ears: *I hope you don't come back.* It suddenly seemed so easy, then, to take Jumbo's words to heart. No one would know, if his plane didn't make it back.

Christ, if it could always be like this, in the sky! The Thames estuary, opening into the great shining plain of the North Sea, unruffled in the calm autumn sunshine, lay below like a map, from the North Foreland up to Orford, where the shingle beach kept the river Alde from joining the sea, the beach from which they had launched their sailing dinghy, he and Jumbo, in the innocent days before war came, when they were friends. They had taken their father and put him at the helm, and the blind man had sailed by feel, as do all good sailors, and not seeing had for once not been a handicap at all. He had laughed and said what good lads they were and he had trusted them and their little dinghy implicitly. It all came back to Chris as he looked down at the rivers and creeks he knew so well from his childhood, the lonely seawalls and the mauve sheets of the sea-lavender across the saltings, the gritty beaches and the wonder of Dunwich, where a whole town had fallen into the sea. How that had amazed them as children! He could see that far, beyond the piers of Clacton and Walton and the tower on the Naze. It was another world from the one he was now used to, yet still just as it was, as magical and peaceful as he always remembered it.

Strangely, it beckoned him farther out to sea. It was asking him to come back. He was low on fuel and knew he should turn back if he was to nurse his plane home, but he flew on. He felt released from fears and guilt. He pushed back the cockpit cover and felt the crisp air flood over him; the sun blinded him. It was wonderful.

The Hurricane limped on, full of bullet holes, dropping gently towards the sea.

Chapter Sixteen

'Where can you go tonight? To one of your friends'? It's too late to go back to your auntie's now. I can go back and sleep in the office, but there's only one camp bed and it's a terrible hole. No place for you.'

Her father was perplexed. They stood on the hospital steps, indecisive. Josie had been turned out but her mother was to stay for a day or two.

'The WVS offered you a place,' he added.

'I'll go to Mary's.'

'You're sure they'll be there?'

'Yes. Unless a bomb dropped on them too.'

'Oh my hat, I still can't believe it! That you weren't both killed! What a terible shock! I don't know what we shall do next. But you can go back to your auntie's until we get sorted out. I expect we can rent somewhere for the time being. As soon as we get settled you can come back again.'

'Yes, that's fine. I'll stay at Mary's tonight and go back tomorrow.'

Back to Chris! Back to Chris! She was ecstatic. Her father looked at her anxiously.

'You're sure you're all right? I'd rather they had kept you in, just for the night. Shock's a funny thing.'

'No, truly, I'm fine.'

'And you can travel up there tomorrow by yourself?'

'Yes, of course. I know the way now.'

Her father gave her three pounds. 'That should see you all right. Tell Betty I'll be in touch as soon as I can. Amazing – the only day you decide to come home and a bomb drops on you! I can't get over it. What a narrow squeak!'

She wanted to say, Stop fussing. She had had a bit of a wash and brushed her hair but she only had the filthy clothes she stood up in, no luggage at all.

'You haven't got a coat . . .'

'It's not cold, and Mary will lend me something if I need it.'

'I shall have to come back tomorrow and see about rescuing our things, what we can. And your mother – we'll have to find somewhere to live. What complications! But, never mind, thank God you're both safe, that's what matters. You're sure you're all right now, on your own?'

'Of course, Dad. I'll go up to Mary's and tomorrow I'll get the train back to Auntie Betty's. It's quite simple.'

'Yes, I forget. You're a grown girl now. All right then. I'll keep you in the picture. Your mother will be dying to get back to work, I know. She thinks the place revolves around her. Maybe it does, I've no idea.'

Josie had never known her father with so much to say. Fuss, fuss, fuss. Perhaps it needed a bomb to shake him out of his habitual silent complacency. He was looking at her as if he had never seen her before. When they parted he gave her an unexpected kiss, only a peck, but a kiss nonetheless.

'Be careful, dear,' were his parting words.

Careful! She hadn't been careful last night! She was so thrilled to be going back to Chris tomorrow that she felt she was sitting on cloud nine. Handing a pound note to the bus conductor for her fare, she was oblivious to his annoyance at having to give her so much change, only staring out of the window as they toiled up the hill, reliving last night. It hadn't been goodbye after all! She couldn't believe her luck.

Mary lived in a smart road off the common. Dear common! She imagined she could still see Chris's wheelmarks on the gravel ride where it came to the roadside. She scrambled down the stairs and hurried away down the wide, leafy road to where Mary's house stood, surrounded by its large garden (hanging out the washing not allowed: this always made Josie giggle). The sun had disappeared and it was sharp, the smell of autumn giving her a lovely feeling – she could not describe it exactly but the change of seasons, even in suburban Wimbledon, always gave her this frisson of joy. The lingering smell of a garden bonfire, the purple blaze of Michaelmas daisies in the border and, at last, clouds in the sky . . . with cloudy, wintry weather

197

the air fighting would be over and Chris would be safe. Chris, oh Chris! She rang the doorbell and jigged with cold on the doorstep. Her day under the rubble was a bad dream. All she could think of was Chris.

'Oh my word, whatever's happened?'

Mary's mother, she of the strange godly beliefs, opened the door cautiously and peered into the dusk.

'Josie! Oh my dear, we haven't seen you for ages! What a strange time to call – is anything wrong? Come in, come in, because of the light. Mind your shoes now. Whatever's happened to you?'

As she switched on the light again, even in its dim gleam she saw a strange apparition for, in spite of the perfunctory clean-up, Josie still looked like a survivor of war, her clothes thick with dust, bits of plaster in her hair.

'Gracious me, you look as if a bomb dropped on you!'

'Yes, it did.'

Her arrival, with her tale to tell, caused consternation in the placid house. Mary came down from her studies, face alight to see Josie again. But there was no chance to talk while her mother fussed over Josie, ran her a bath, found her some clean clothes, made her beans on toast, and got her to tell the whole story of her incarceration. Both Mary's parents were full of concern. By the time she was clean and fed and the excitement was abating, Josie began to feel shaky and weird.

'You must go to bed. You must be suffering from

shock after all that. You're very pale. What you want now is a good night's sleep.'

She had scarcely slept at all the night before. Now she lay in the luxurious comfort of the guest-room bed, in a large, close-carpeted bedroom with pink curtains and religious pictures on the walls, but no sleep was forthcoming. She never wanted to sleep while she could just lie there and remember dancing with Chris's arms round her, his lips tickling her hair, kissing the nape of her neck. She had to tell Mary: her own real Biggles, who loved her.

But Mary was at her door already, coming to see if she was awake.

'No, I was just coming to look for you. I can't sleep.'

'No, it's been such ages since we met. School is so boring without you, and hardly anyone there. They've nearly all been evacuated.'

'I couldn't bear to be still at school. It must be awful.'

'Yes, when so much is going on. I want to join up when I'm old enough.'

'What, the air force? Be a WAAF? Oh Mary, I have to tell you – I've met a pilot, a fighter pilot—'

And it all spilled out, what she had never been able to tell anyone, what she had kept to herself for so long – or was it long, really? She could hardly remember the time before she loved Chris. Mary was agog, poor scar-faced Mary who had never been out with a boy yet but with her vivid imagination had dreams just as Josie had had dreams.

199

'Oh, how wonderful! Fancy being right next to the airfield! Seeing it all under your nose. I thought it was going to be so boring for you up there!'

'Yes, well, it is, living in the country. But it's all right if there's someone – oh, listen, I must tell you too. There's something awful as well.'

And she explained how she had met Jumbo and thought she was in love with him until she met his brother.

'And then I had to tell him I was going with Chris. It was terrible.'

'And he loves you too?'

'Yes.'

'They're fighting over you?' Mary's eyes shone.

'Well, no, not really. But it's rather awful for Jumbo. I don't feel very good about it. But I suppose it happens all the time.'

She tried to dismiss it, but even as she said the words she hated herself for her flippancy. For Jumbo wasn't just any hanging-in-there boy, wanting her for what he could get: he was very special, not someone to be damaged. She had tried to shut this thought away every time it came near, but it was hard. She was ashamed.

But Mary, in spite of being ignorant of the pangs of love, was far more perceptive about Josie's plight than dumb Maureen would have been. It was such a relief to talk to a friend again: Mary understood everything. She snuggled in under the eiderdown and they whispered, giggled, despaired, reminisced, until the heavy grandfather clock in the hall downstairs struck midnight. A cold full moon shone in through the window. Josie suddenly felt very tired. What a strange day!

'How lucky you've been!' Mary whispered enviously.

It was the best way of looking at it: not dead, from the bomb; being loved by two brothers . . . but it was not all happiness. When Mary had crept away, Josie fell asleep with the astonishing memory of her mother reciting poetry in her ear, the last thing she would ever have expected of her: 'When I am dead, my dearest, Sing no sad songs for me . . .'

Her mother! Perhaps one day she would learn to know her parents.

Chapter Seventeen

Jumbo stood resting on his crutches, looking out of the long windows of the hospital dayroom. He knew he wasn't going to enjoy this visit very much, but at least being here at last was what he wanted most in the world. It was too early to have made friends, although most of the inmates seemed to be young like himself. Unlike himself, though, they were nearly all servicemen, and he felt his civilian status undermining. Only a motorbike idiot, after all – he could hardly explain so soon that he had actually joined the air force before the accident happened.

It was late afternoon and the evening sun was fierce. On the green lawns he was looking out on groups of men, some with nurses, several alone, trying to exercise their shattered bodies. Some had terrible burns as well as amputations; some walked easily but had only one arm; some had one leg and were practising with the new prosthetic, which he knew would be himself in a day or two. It did not look easy, even though they were perhaps the least maimed of the men he looked down upon. It took time, he knew that. But at least he was starting. He dwelled on his luck in getting a place here at last – anything to stave off the memory of his parting from the two people he loved the most. In his anger he hadn't made a good job of it. It seared him now, just when he had what he most wanted.

He would ring Chris at the airfield in another hour and take back what he had said. As for Josie – there was no sorting that out. If she loved Chris, there was no hope for him, and he knew she couldn't change it even if she wanted to.

A bee beat its way up the long window. He wanted to let it out but there was no way, unless it got to the top and the opening. He was always rescuing birds and insects, even worms. Stupid really. If his leg was a success and he got into the air force he would have more on his plate than the rescuing of worms. The last few months had been terrible, only made possible by Josie. Thank God she hadn't met Chris any earlier.

He wasn't sure what to do, where to go. He could do with some tea and knew there was a mess somewhere, but didn't know where. As he turned away to go looking, a nurse came up to him and said, 'Is your name Patterson?'

'Yes.'

'A phone call came for you. From your mother. She wants you to get in touch. There's a phone box in the hall.'

'Thank you. I'll go down.'

Was she fussing to see that he had settled in? It wasn't like her. But, he supposed, it was probably a thing all mothers did, even his. When he thought about it, which he very rarely did, he supposed she dreaded his going into the air force, like Chris.

He hopped down the stairs to the entrance hall and saw the public phone inside the door. He found the right money and dialled his home number. Probably she was waiting for him to ring back. Yes, she answered almost at once.

'Jumbo! Are you all right?'

'Of course I'm all right.'

'I don't know if I'm doing the right thing telling you this, but I think you should be prepared for bad news. You would want to know, I'm sure. It's Chris.'

He could not answer.

'He didn't come back this morning. He's missing. Nobody saw what happened, nobody saw him shot down, so it's early days yet. We mustn't lose heart. It's happened before, you know that.'

'Yes.'

All Jumbo could think of were his last words to Chris: *I wouldn't care if you never came back.*

Now he knew what a lie that was. He cared. Christ, he cared!

'Are you all right, Jumbo? I know it's a dreadful shock for you. I wish you were still here at home.'

'I'm all right,' he lied.

'I'll let you know as soon as there's any more news. Be brave, dear. It's come at a very bad time for you.'

'OK, Ma. Thanks for ringing me.'

As if it was just a bit of gossip. I must tell you this . . .

He put the phone down before she could fuss. He stood very still, looking out of the doors at the people coming and going.

He let out a terrible cry. 'Chris, I didn't mean it! I didn't mean it!'

Then he stood there screaming until the staff came running and hustled him away and, quite soon, stuck a needle in him and put him to bed.

Chapter Eighteen

Josie left Mary's house as soon as she decently could without being rude. Mary came with her to the bus stop. Her mother had insisted on giving her a bag of sandwiches and a bottle of lemonade, and a spare jacket of Mary's. 'You can post it back, dear. You can't go on a long journey like that without a coat.' Josie bumped it against her legs, hurrying for the main road.

'Aren't you going to see your mother before you go?' Mary asked.

Josie hadn't thought of it.

'She's all right. There's nothing wrong with her. She's going back to work as soon as she gets out.'

'Are you coming back afterwards, when you've got somewhere else to live? To go to the art school?'

'I don't know!'

At that moment Josie felt wild horses wouldn't drag her away from Chris again. She couldn't bear it. But she knew she was being slightly mad.

'I don't know what I'm going to do!' Save get on that train, hurry, hurry back . . .

'Write to me! Tell me what happens to your Biggles!' Mary shouted after her as the bus bore her away.

It was a soft, hazy autumn day with a smell of rain, the clouds coming and going. Perhaps too cloudy to fly. Come lower, clouds, Josie prayed, shut out the bright sky, keep dear Chris safe on the ground. Perhaps it was the effects of yesterday, but she felt light-headed and a bit sick. She was all to pieces, not in the calm Patterson mode. Perhaps she would only have a few days back at Auntie Betty's if her father found them somewhere to live. They would expect her to start at the art school. The threat of invasion that had sent her away was over now; nobody thought it was going to happen any more and life would continue as usual, bombs or no bombs. But how could life continue as usual? It was impossible. Her life was out of control.

She caught the train into London and crossed to Liverpool Street. There were no Dunkirk veterans around this time but plenty of soldiers and airmen looking spruce and cheerful. The stink of defeat was absent. The Luftwaffe had been repulsed and talk was of Hitler abandoning his plans to invade. The atmosphere in London was all bustle and optimism, with just as many crowds on the streets as there always had been. It was strange how, with their backs to the wall, people were suddenly more friendly, more joky.

Josie found it hard to believe that only yesterday she had been lying under the rubble of her house. Her past life was now wiped out: all her old toys, her teddy-bear, her art work in its neat folders, her box of what she called jewels, her scrapbooks, her Biggles books, her china rabbit: all her dearest things were now scattered in the rubble, open to the sky. She should have gone back and helped her father pick over the mess. But the ruin had been cordoned off even before she had been rescued. They wouldn't let her in now; it would be too dangerous. So much for possessions. Travel light – one of Jumbo's mottoes. There wasn't really anything she felt grief for. The china rabbit, if anything. How stupid! What mattered was where she was going, not where she had been. To Chris. Tonight was her night in the pub. Jumbo was still away, as far as she knew. She would see Chris tonight!

The train was crowded and incredibly slow. It kept stopping for no visible reason, panting clouds of smoke. The sky was empty. Josie did not know that impatience could be so consuming; it was impossible to keep still. She wriggled her way out into the corridor and stood with her nose pressed to the window. Miles of stubble, cows, emptiness . . . oh, *please*, train, get a move on! It trickled forward, jerked, stopped again. Josie wanted to scream.

An hour late, it eventually steamed into Josie's station and she tumbled out, clutching her bag. She knew there would be no one to meet her – they couldn't know she was coming, after all, but there was a bus in half an hour that would take her most of the way. She sat on a bench, drinking her lemonade, waiting. The minute hand on the station clock scarcely moved, as if the world had gone to sleep. A few cows came past, herded by two boys, then a Ferguson tractor, two old cars . . . some women with shopping. And then two more came to wait with her at the bus stop, an encouraging sign. When the bus came, the driver knew her from her trips to the cinema with Jumbo, and gave her a grin . . . at last she was underway again!

It was well into the afternoon by the time she got there. A Hurricane came in to land as she got off the bus, but it wasn't Chris's. She ran up the lane, not stopping even for the stitch, and panted round to the kitchen door. Auntie Betty was taking some washing off the line, and cried out when she saw her.

'Oh my God, you're safe, you're safe! Bert went to meet you but got tired of waiting – I told him he was stupid to come back, but he said he'd got too much work to do to spend all day at the station. What a crazy thing, to go home and get a bomb on you – I can't believe it! Your father sent us a telegram this morning to say you were coming back. And poor old Edna – what a shock! So how are you? All in one piece? Tell me what happened! The telegram just said, "House bombed. All safe. Josie returning today." What happened?'

Josie had to explain. It seemed to take for ever. When Bert came in she had to say it all over again.

'Buried in the rubble, eh? That was a close squeak then, that you weren't killed. Well, perhaps it's safer up here after all. We haven't had any more bombs.'

'There, Bert, you should have waited longer for that wretched train. You must be so tired, Josie, after such a shock. It will be early to bed for you tonight.'

'No, I'm quite all right now! It's my night down at the pub.'

'Surely not tonight, dear. You can give it a miss – Albert thinks you're in London anyway.'

'They might not be in tonight, those young men,' Bert said. 'They took a beating yesterday. Two didn't come back and this morning another one. That's four in just three days. They say they're moving out to-morrow, going somewhere up north for a rest.'

'Who didn't come back?' Josie's voice shook.

'I dunno who it was. I don't know them by name. It's only what I heard on the farm.'

'And they're going away?'

Josie could not trust herself to ask any more. Telling Mary was the only time she had had a chance to put her crazy feelings into words, spilling them out in tangled confusion under the eiderdown with her friend. Nobody up here knew anything about the love that flared between Chris and herself, only poor Jumbo. And he was unlikely to tell anyone, after all. Even now, with Uncle Bert's frightening news, she had to keep her cool. Three pilots gone, after Peter! How could she find out if one of them was Chris?

'I'd rather go down to the pub. It keeps me busy. I

suppose another squadron will take their place – Albert will know.'

'Well, I suppose you're feeling all at sixes and sevens. It won't do any harm. Maureen's gone to the pictures with Tom.'

'Did she work at the big house today? Does she know if one of the pilots was Jumbo's brother?'

'No. It was her day at Stratton's today. Why, I hadn't thought, perhaps one of them is the Patterson boy. Oh my word, that would be terrible!'

Josie had to stay talking in the kitchen while Auntie Betty boiled her an egg and made toast. She could feel herself shaking, on the point of breaking down, but she forced herself to hold on, not show anything. The effort was crucifying. Not to know, that was the worst thing of all.

'Why, you do look peaky,' Betty exclaimed as she put the egg before her. 'I think you'd best be in bed early tonight.'

'No, I shall never sleep. I must find out – because of Jumbo . . . it would be so awful for him if his brother's missing.'

'Yes, they're very close, the boys. Poor Jumbo if it is – he's enough to put up with without losing his brother.'

Josie thought the egg would choke her. She forced herself to eat: the sooner she could escape up to her room the better. Thank heavens Maureen was out.

'I'll go up and sort out some clothes. I lost all the stuff I took with me.'

'Gracious, I hadn't thought of that. I think they give you more coupons if you lose stuff in a raid – so I've read somewhere. We'll have to find out about it.'

Josie escaped. Bert had turned the radio on and the news was all about how many bombers had been shot down, how many fighters were missing. 'The tide has turned at last,' someone was quoted as saying. 'The German losses far outnumber our own.' Josie ran. She flung herself on her bed and pulled the pillow over her head and sobbed.

'No, Chris, not you, Chris! Please God, not Chris!'

His parting words: *It's all over for us, Josie,* came back to her like a physical blow. She had purposefully shut them away all this time. Now she knew that he had meant it: first, because he was physically going away on leave, and then the squadron was being moved; second, because she was Jumbo's girl, not his; and third because he thought he was unlikely to survive. How could it be any different? She knew now that he was ashamed of what he had done in loving her, that it had not made him happy, only made him despair. Wrapped up completely in her own feelings, she had not stopped to consider his.

It was very hard to pull herself together, stop her stupid crying. She was crying for the moon, after all, she knew that now. If only he was safe, that was all she wanted now, to know that. No more. She had to go and find out.

It was a cold evening. When she went down to the pub the air was crisp, the stars just coming out.

The pub was quiet, just three regulars, elderly men. She went into the kitchen, where Albert was pottering about.

'Why, I thought you'd gone home. I wasn't expecting you.'

'No, I came back because my house got bombed. I just came to see if – my auntie said there were casualties amongst the boys . . . I wondered who. I thought you would know. Will they come in tonight?'

'I don't know. They're all flying off north tomorrow and we get a new lot in. Yes, it was a bad day yesterday. Two of them, the one they call Mac – he was shot down and killed, and the Patterson boy is missing. No one knows what happened to him. They're still hoping he'll turn up.'

So, her dread was realized. A great icy hand seemed to settle on her, squeezing her heart dry. The calamity that had been hanging over her, every day, it seemed for ever, was reported by the publican in unexcited tones.

Missing. Not knowing was almost worse than a clean report of death.

She forced herself to speak. 'Was that yesterday, when he went missing?'

'Yes, the first patrol. He didn't come back. Just when he'd got to be squadron leader too, after his pal copped it the day before. It's been a dreadful week. We all feel it, in the village.'

The first patrol, just a few hours after they had said goodbye. *It's all over for us, Josie.* What had he done?

213

Not cared, not had Peter to watch out for him, not been clever enough? Not wanted to go on living?

'I just wanted to know.'

Well, now she knew. But missing was an enigma. They often turned up, the fighter boys, after being reported missing. It meant nobody actually saw them crash or get destroyed. They could crash-land, unseen, or bale out over the sea and get picked up and not report in for a few days. They could parachute down and lie unconscious in a wood. They could abscond. But most likely they crashed and their plane was found in a distant place some days later – though if it was into the sea, it was never found, not ever. As Chris was often out over the estuary and the North Sea this last was the most likely. What had he told her? *Hurricanes don't float.*

She felt strange now, distanced, as if her whole affair with Chris had been a dream. Her feelings were frozen. No more crying: there were people to see her, to notice an excess of grief. She could show only moderate grief, for her boyfriend's brother. Seemly. No histrionics.

But she was emptied of emotion now. She fled the pub and stumbled away into the darkness. She told herself that she had always known what was going to happen, but she had always pushed the knowledge away. She hadn't wanted to know. That was true. Facing it now, it did not come as a shock. She walked slowly home, not stopping at the gateway where he had kissed her. She wanted her bed, oblivion. Her mind was blank, her body frozen.

* * *

'Look, there's a letter from your father this morning, Josie. He says can you stay here just for another week – then from next Saturday he's got the lease of a flat and you can go back and settle down again. Your mother's out of hospital and right as rain. That's good news, isn't it? My word, what a narrow squeak you both had! No wonder you look so poorly, my poor girl. Here's a cup of tea, sit down.'

Fuss, fuss. Josie sat down. Across the table Maureen stared at her suspiciously.

She said, 'Chris Patterson is missing. Did you know?'

'Yes, I found out last night.'

'I clean there today. It'll be awful.'

'Is Jumbo back?'

'I don't know.'

'He's bound to come back now his brother is missing,' said Auntie Betty. 'A family needs to be together at times like this.'

Bert said, 'I don't know. This hospital thing is very important to him – he's waited long enough. There's nothing for them to do at home, after all, no funeral or anything.'

'He might come back yet,' said Auntie Betty. 'It's only two days.'

It felt like for ever.

'It's a terrible thing for them.'

It's a terrible thing for me . . . Josie could see no way how she could exist sanely for a whole week here with nothing to do save think about Chris. She had to get

215

away, be by herself. She made some excuse to Auntie Betty and went off down the lane. Maureen hurried after her, on her way to work, not what Josie had intended. Maureen wasn't due at Nightingales for another half-hour.

'So who are you missing most, Chris or Jumbo?' she asked with the suggestion of a sneer.

'Both.'

'It's Chris, isn't it? You're barmy about him. I saw you.'

'It didn't mean anything. He was giving me a lift, just trying it on.'

'You were enjoying it, what I saw.'

'Yes, you would've too! It didn't mean anything, not to him. Don't be stupid.'

'You could fool me.'

'Well, just shut up about it. Or I'll tell the whole village you're pregnant.'

'I'm not! I started a couple of days ago. Gosh, what a relief! I nearly died of happiness.'

'Bully for you!'

'Well, look, I'm not going to say anything about you and Chris. Keep your hair on. I'm sorry about him, it's awful. If I find anything out at the house I'll let you know.'

'Yes, well, it's Jumbo I care about,' Josie lied. 'It will be terrible for him.'

'OK. See you later.'

Maureen turned away to take the footpath across the field towards the big house, and Josie turned instinctively for the lake. As she did so there was a roar of engines and eight Hurricanes came over, taking off. Josie stood and watched. They were in formation: two Vs of three and two behind, the remains of the squadron of twelve. The flew away to the north, making a big curve, and Josie could picture the pilots' relief and joy, hear their banter on the intercom, think of their anticipation of hours of unbroken sleep, the celebration in the mess, the drinking. If Chris had been one of them she knew now that she could have borne his departure, knowing that he was flying to safety. Before, she had thought it would be the end of the world. If only! Nothing was as stark as 'Missing'. It was death really, but death hedged about with dreadful uncertainties, which made it worse.

She took the familiar path across the fields and through the woods to the lake. Across the expanse of water the ruined house stood against the skyline, silent and deserted as always. There was no wind and the trees hung still. The bird calls came clearly, the woodpecker and the moorhens and the twittering of all the little brown things she could not name. She remembered Chris saying that Peter knew them all. She skirted round the lake on the beaten track the wild animals had made and came to the erstwhile lawn. As she walked slowly up towards the house she found she was following the gouged marks in the grass where Chris had landed his plane. How strange, that first meeting! If they had not met in that magical way there might never have been a love affair at all.

She went and sat on what had once been the French window steps leading to the lawn. Nothing changed here, the place cocooned in decay, slipping year by year a little further into oblivion. It too had lost its guardian in war, was left desolate, like herself. It was comforting, somehow, to be in this place where Chris had spent his childhood, had crashed his plane, had met her. Jumbo had said that one day he would like to buy it and make it come to life again. What dreams! Dreams were all that was left now. Poor Jumbo! She was not the only one devastated by Chris's disappearance.

After a while she got cold, and knew that she had to accept what had happened and try to seem normal. Nobody must know how she felt. She had to appear sad for her boyfriend's brother, not devastated by the loss of a lover. She walked home slowly, getting back in control, the worst of the shock over now. If she appeared sad, it was the after-effect of having a bomb dropped on her, no more.

She existed in a sort of coma for two days, until a letter came for her in the post. Auntie Betty was treating her with kid gloves, thinking she was suffering from the after-effects of being bombed, kindness itself. She brought the letter to her when she came down to breakfast.

'It's from London. I don't know the writing. It's not from your mother.'

She had probably held it up to the light and pored over the postmark. The markings said Richmond, so

Josie knew it was from Jumbo. She opened it nervously.

Dearest Josie,

I don't feel like writing much, not after our awful parting. I expect you know by now that Chris has been reported missing. I should have gone home immediately but the hospital wouldn't let me, and I think it was for the best as I have my new leg and am being taught how to use it. What good would I be at home? I ache for you as much as for myself, but cannot put my feelings into words. My mother told me on the phone that her sister and husband are coming down from Scotland and there will be a dinner for them on Friday and I must be there. I am writing to ask you to come too. I can't face this without you, it will be so awful. I dread coming home. Can you forget how cruelly I spoke to you? I know now that you love Chris and I will not put upon you, but just as a friend, Josie, I need you. I know you are going home shortly and just hope this letter reaches you in time at your aunt's. The dinner is at seven. Please do come. I have told my mother to expect you.

 Yours, as ever, J.

There was no way of refusing such an invitation, but Josie was horrified at the thought of it. To see Jumbo again would be difficult enough, but to sit with his family, pretending to them all that she had scarcely known Chris – as they thought – was going to be an ordeal akin to torture. And to face Jumbo again . . . it didn't bear thinking about.

Auntie Betty was so nosy, obviously dying to know what the letter was about, that Josie read the gist of it to her, the part that invited her to dinner.

'Oh my word, in that smart set and under such circumstances – it won't be a very happy party, will it? Do you want to go?'

'No, I don't.'

'But – poor boy! I think you must, the way he puts it. He's obviously very fond of you, dear. You must help him – he was very close to his brother. They were inseparable as boys, we all knew that. It will be desperate for him if Chris is dead.'

'Yes, I know. I will go, of course.'

She had to turn away to hide her feelings. But it was good practice. This is how it must be, she told herself. Dead-pan. Poor Chris, my boyfriend's brother.

'I suppose you must have been the last to see him – Chris, I mean, when he drove you home. Did Edna meet him, or did he just put you down outside the door?'

'He just dropped me outside.'

'And then the next morning – first patrol, they said, and he was gone.' She was bustling about, getting the dinner. Bert came in at one. Josie, head down, laid out the knives and forks. 'I wonder what happened to him? They think he was shot down over the sea.'

'He might have been picked up. He might turn up.'

But Josie knew he wouldn't, even as she spoke. Hurricanes don't float. Parachute and you drown. Going straight in kills you quicker. The impact kills you.

'Oh, here's Maureen. She might have some news.'

Josie looked up quickly, her heart giving a bound, but all Maureen had to say was, 'Well, you'd think all was quite normal up there. The old girl reading her *Horse and Hound*, the old boy off to London as usual. She didn't say much though, hardly noticed I was there. Some relatives are coming to stay. I had to get the rooms ready, try and reduce the dust layer, clean some silver. Not a word about Chris.'

'Our Josie's been asked to supper on Friday. She got a letter from Jumbo.'

'Oh, that's nice for her.' Maureen's eyes gleamed. 'Can't say as it's going to be very jolly though, in the circumstances.'

'I don't want to go.'

'I bet you don't!'

Auntie Betty gave her daughter a curious look. 'Why? It will be lovely for her to see Jumbo again. You must have missed him, Josie?'

'Yes, I did.'

Maureen was a loose cannon, making her ambiguous remarks. When they were alone Josie said to her, 'If you make any remarks to anyone about me and Chris, I told you, I'll tell your mother you thought you were pregnant.'

'Crikey, don't do that!'

'Well then, mind what you say. It's not fair, not for me or him. Just a kiss that night – it was nothing. He'd been drinking. What would you have done?'

'Lordy, I'd have been in heaven! He's so smashing!'

Josie had to smile at that, in spite of everything.

The long hours stretched ahead. She longed now to be away, back in Wimbledon, starting at the art college, her head full of new ideas to crowd out the thoughts that tortured her. The sky was silent, the autumn sun gilded the pale stubble and Uncle Bert's cows grazed peacefully. No one would ever have known there was a war on.

She had to fish out something to wear at Nightingales, to look up to standard. She hadn't shopped for ages and had quite a lot of coupons but her heart wasn't in it. What did it matter what she looked like? She went out in the garden and dug furiously where Uncle Bert had started, hoping to tire herself out, but the earth was dry and easy to dig and all she achieved was some blisters which Auntie Betty diligently pierced and treated with iodine, which made her scream.

Chapter Nineteen

Jumbo came home from London in his father's car. He had come out of hospital because he knew his parents wanted him, but it was at the worst possible time, when the difficulties of adjusting to his new leg were scarcely started, much less overcome. The hospital said it would get better. It couldn't get worse, in Jumbo's opinion, and he was only grateful that his blind father could not see the state he was in. Thank God he still had his crutches with him.

'Your mother needs you,' his father said tersely. 'I don't like to leave her all day, but my work demands it. If you can just see her through a few days it would help all round. I put off asking you, I know the situation you're in, but there – it has to be. I knew you'd understand.'

'Yes, I'd have come anyway. But I had to wait to get signed out. They're working overtime down there.'

'It's not come as a great shock, after all, as I suppose at the back of our minds we always knew it could happen at any time. But of course that doesn't soften the blow.'

'No. There's no more news, I suppose?'

'No. No word, save it's pretty certain he was over the sea, so that's not very encouraging.'

'How's Ma taking it?'

'How do you expect? She's very calm.'

More than he was, no doubt, Jumbo thought, not wanting to relive his breakdown when the news had reached the hospital. Another thank God, that he had not had his parents as witnesses. The hospital people had been kindness itself, with drugs for oblivion as well as for pain. But now he just had to get through the next few days as best he could, living up to his parents' code, before he could bolt back to the comradely arms of the prosthetics workshops.

'Your leg giving you gyp?'

'Yes, it is rather.'

'They say it takes a bit of getting used to.'

'More than I expected, yes. The inflammation – it gets worse rather than better.'

'Give it time. You always were the impatient one.'

'Yes, that's what I tell myself.'

'Bad days all round. It will get better. Even losing Chris. He was doing what he wanted.'

'It's still what I want too.'

'Good man.'

It was getting near dusk when the car arrived home. Jumbo glanced at his watch, remembering he had said seven to Josie. He owed it to her to be there when she arrived, knowing how nervous she was of his parents. Not without reason: they scared the pants off him. That was his greatest bond with Chris: the effort to live up to what was expected; why they had gone on those wild, mad expeditions together, to let off steam. Missing him was like the other leg gone: he was cut down. His greatest dread realized. There were no words to express the feeling of loss.

He stumbled out of the car, gasping with pain as the false leg took the weight. He must get it off, he would never get through the night otherwise. But that meant finding some one-legged trousers. Getting upstairs to his bedroom would finish him off . . .

'Darling, I'm so glad you were able to come!'

His mother stood on the steps, smiling. Dressed in her classic dinner-party clothes, she looked magnificent. She kissed her husband and waited for Jumbo to follow her in. He just wanted to stand there and bawl like a baby, for Chris, for his pain, for his world falling apart. But no, he limped in, using his crutches, smiling. Chris got a medal for less than this, he thought, clenching his teeth.

But his Aunt Eunice and Uncle Robert – his mother's sister and her husband, a Scottish banker – were there to greet them, and pleasantries were exchanged. He managed to hold up until, thank God, they repaired into the sitting room for drinks and he was able to disengage his crucifying leg in the downstairs loo, leave it in the washing basket in the scullery and hop upstairs for his old trousers. The pain still throbbed from his stump but it was now bearable, more bearable than anything else that he expected to happen that evening. Poor Josie, he *had* landed her in it! Perhaps she wouldn't come. Perhaps she had already gone back home: he didn't know what she had been up to lately. But his mother didn't say there had been any message. She knew Josie had been invited; he had told her on the telephone. He didn't think she was pleased, from the sound of her voice, but that was something else. He needed Josie now, more than ever, even if she didn't love him any more.

Josie walked up the drive on the dot of seven, feeling that she was pushing one leg in front of the other with an iron will, so reluctant did she feel. She was cursing herself for not pretending she was still in Wimbledon. Jumbo did not know her movements of late and nobody knew of her own recent adventures, unless it had got to Nightingales on the village grapevine. Maureen hadn't told Mrs Patterson, she knew. No words had been exchanged during Maureen's tour of duty, save about cleaning up the spare bedroom. Maureen said she hadn't even dared to say sorry to her employer, about Chris, so scary was her demeanour. And as for meeting Jumbo again, after Chris, Josie had no idea now what her feelings were. She was mad to come!

When she saw Jumbo again she was stricken by his pale, dishevelled looks. His face was gaunt, and beneath his tired eyes the skin was as if bruised, blueish-grey. She stepped into the hall and he

226

dropped his crutches and put his arms round her, hugging her close.

'Josie, my Josie, I'm so glad you've come.'

So then she was glad too, because his pain was so palpable, but she knew she didn't love him any more.

'I thought you had a new leg?'

'I've left it in the scullery. It's killing me.'

'Oh, Jumbo, I'm so sorry!'

Sorry about everything. Words were useless. He took it to mean Chris and said, 'Yes, the worst. What we all dreaded.'

'Is there any hope?'

'Not now. Very unlikely.'

'It's terrible.' Her voice shook and she pulled away, desperate to stay calm. Fortunately Mrs Patterson came out into the hall to greet her and she was able to pull herself together. The woman smiled as if everything was just as usual.

'My dear, I'm so glad you could come,' she said. Josie knew she was lying through her teeth.

'Thank you. I'm so sorry about Chris.' Rising to the Patterson protocol, she found her voice was now quite steady. She could do it too. Cover up, lie, pretend, put on an act.

'Yes. It helps a lot now Jumbo's come, and you too. Come and meet my sister and her husband. They've come down from Edinburgh. Family matters at times like this.'

Not much hugging and kissing going on, even if it was family. Mrs Patterson's sister Eunice was a woman

227

in the same mould, not nearly so handsome but with a steely, intelligent eye, introduced as Dr Campbell. She had grey hair pulled back in a bun, but lack of expertise allowed untidy strands to fall over her ears and forehead, which gave her a slightly dotty look. She looked like some sort of intellectual don, not a GP. Her husband Robert looked like a hunting, shooting and fishing sort of man, with a florid red face, thinning ginger hair and a rather strange tweed suit.

Nobody was talking about Chris and they all seemed quite jolly. Josie stood apart with Jumbo and was given a glass of wine. She was frightened to drink it, knowing what it did to her brains, and stood twisting it in her hands. She asked Jumbo about his leg and he told her, mostly about the technical bits.

'It's not an overnight thing, though. It takes ages for it to be comfortable, but you just have to go through with it, toughening up the stump. I took it off tonight, I couldn't stand it any more. Not with all this too. Brain pain.' He was keeping his voice down. 'I shouldn't have asked you. It was just, coming back here, knowing that Chris was gone – I couldn't face it. But I had to, and I thought having you would help, in spite of how we parted. I've regretted that. We are still friends, after all.'

'I'm going home tomorrow.'

Josie tried to smile as once she would have done, but her face felt frozen. They were talking about Chris now, drifting towards the dinner table where Tilly was setting down the dishes. She wanted to listen.

'He was low on fuel, they said, but he wouldn't turn back, which is rather strange.'

'His pal Peter was killed the day before. You don't know how it affects . . . they were very close.'

'One soldiers on, there's no alternative in war.'

'Oh, but they're so young! Scarcely out of school. It's asking so much.'

'No, that's the age when they can do it. No fears, no cares about family, all in it together – a sort of sport really. Like riding point-to-point on a crazy thorough-bred. The young have no nerves.'

Josie had seen how Chris's hand shook, known about his nightmares, seen the nervous tic by his mouth. No, he had shown no sign of nerves. Only in parts he couldn't control.

'His birthday was just coming up. He would have been twenty at the end of the month.'

'Well, a short life, but he certainly lived it. Not like so many poor beggars who join up to escape the bore-dom. You couldn't say that of Chris.'

The old bore turned to Jumbo and said, 'You shared it with him too, until he did for you with that leg. What are you up to now? What's the future for you?'

'I'm going to join the air force and be a pilot like Chris.'

'How's that possible, for heaven's sake? They'll never let you fly, surely?'

'There's a pilot flying on active service who lost both his legs several years ago. Not just one leg but two. So why can't I?'

Jumbo's voice was very calm, very sure. Old Robert looked astonished.

'I think willpower comes into it. If you want it enough,' Jumbo's father said. 'Both the boys have that.'

They were taking their seats at the table, where everything was arrayed in shining order. Josie remembered how Maureen spoke of slaving over the silver. Why hadn't Chris turned back? she was thinking.

There was roast beef. Another errant heifer, Josie wondered.

'Will you carve, sir?' Tilly asked the colonel, and guided his hands so tactfully to the knife and fork and then the knife to the side of the roast. Years of practice on both their parts, of willpower on his, to do what he had always done. He carved beautifully.

'I don't know how you do it, Mike,' said Robert.

Josie guessed the admiration would have been better not expressed for she saw Mrs Patterson wince sightly. The colonel said nothing. Tilly passed the vegetables.

'They're all out of the garden – Percy's good work,' Mrs Patterson said. 'He's a marvel.'

Josie didn't know how she could get the food down. Every mouthful stuck in her throat. Washing it down with the wine wasn't going to help. She sat between Robert and Jumbo. Jumbo said nothing at all and Robert addressed her, if at all, as a schoolgirl, in a patronizing voice. Watching, listening, she saw nothing to suggest that this wasn't a perfectly ordinary dinner party, without any kind of trauma. If Chris's name came into the conversation it was as if he still existed. Nobody showed grief or pain. To Josie it was totally unreal. She had expected an emotional wake, even from these cold, tight people. She didn't think she could last the night out, buttoning herself into silence. Every time she looked at Mrs Patterson she saw Chris's eyes and, fleetingly, his expressions, the curve of his mouth in her smile, sometimes even an inflexion in her voice. Her whole being shook with her love for him, her pain at his loss. Josie had never guessed such pain could exist.

'Of course,' Mrs Patterson was saying, 'Peter's death the day before must have affected him. It must have been a terrible blow. They were very close. He was going to spend his leave climbing with Peter, not here at home with us. He told us on the phone. We were very disappointed.'

'Peter was a fine chap,' her husband said. 'I think a steadying influence. Very brainy, like his father. His father had a chair in classics at Oxford, and he was a damned fine shot, so I believe. Not often those brainy chaps go in for a proper sport, only squash and such-like. And Peter liked shooting too. It must have counted for something when it came to aiming at Huns, all his practice with pheasants, a moving target. It's a pity Chris didn't do more. It would have stood him in good stead. Chris was too impatient to stand waiting, that was his trouble.'

'It's a terrible waste, losing young men of that

calibre,' said Robert. 'The country will need them after the war.'

What snobs they were, Josie thought angrily. Losing silly oily Sidney would be just as much a waste in the motorbike world, even if he had no brains. His mother would weep no less; in fact she would weep far more than the ice-maiden who was poor Chris's mother.

Tilly came in to clear the plates and, on an impulse, seeing she had so much to carry, Josie got up to help her. She knew immediately from Mrs Patterson's expression that it was not proper behaviour but the conversation was so painful she wanted an excuse to escape. She took all the plates in a pile, while Tilly scooped up the serving dishes.

In the kitchen Tilly turned to her and said, 'There, dear, don't fret. They can't help being how they are.'

'I can't bear it!'

'No. It's their way of getting through it, to put on a brave front. It's how we were taught when we were little, you see, my generation and theirs.'

'I didn't want to come. Jumbo made me.' She started to cry helplessly. Tilly came round to the sink and put her homely arms round her.

'There, dear. I know how you feel. I loved him too, like he was my own boy, and when I'm up there in my room I cry my heart out. If she hears me I don't care. I raised him and poor Jumbo too, more than their own mother did. I'm talking out of turn – it's just between you and me, girl, because we feel the same. I know how you ache inside. Me too.'

She started to cry as well and then, as if the thought struck them both at the same time, they pulled apart and started to laugh instead.

'If she comes in and finds us! Bless my soul!'

They were close to hysteria. Tilly mopped her eyes. 'Love a duck, what a pair we are! Get a grip, darling, we've got the pud to serve. But no, you'd better go back. No hobnobbing with the servants. You're a guest.'

'I want to go home!'

'Just see it out, for Jumbo's sake. Poor boy, he's the one I'm really sorry for. You can be a great help to him, he's so fond of you. Try not to break his heart, he's taking Chris's death so hard. Come on, blow your nose.'

She held out her handkerchief and mopped up Josie's tears.

'Off you go.'

Josie left her, trailing across the hall in a daze. Would this evening never end? She slipped back into her seat, unremarked upon. The conversation was now quite lighthearted, dwelling on the scrapes Chris and Jumbo had got into in their schoolboy years. Jumbo, bravely trying to show willing, said, 'And those are only the ones you know about!' A fair intake of wine was helping the evening along. Soon they would all be laughing. Under the tablecloth she groped for Jumbo's hand. She found it, and felt his response. He was on her side. When Robert was recounting some stupid memory in a loud voice

Jumbo whispered, 'I couldn't have done this if you hadn't been here.'

'What would you have done?'

'Hidden in my room. Locked the door, refused to come out.'

'She'd have shot the lock off.'

They both laughed. Josie thought she was going to have hysterics again. But luckily Tilly came back in with the pudding plates and then on another journey with an amazing meringue thing and a jug of cream.

'How do you do it, with a war on?' Eunice exclaimed. 'You really must have a friend in the black market!'

'No, a friend on a farm, that's all. We don't suffer in the country, not like you town dwellers. We have our own hens, after all. Thank you, Tilly.'

Josie met Tilly's glance and giggled. Tilly winked. Were they all mad? Was Chris laughing, up in heaven?

Mrs Patterson stood up to slice into the meringue.

She said, 'Such a lovely man gave us a ring this morning – people are so kind!'

Her gaze removed itself from the meringue and landed on Josie, who was watching in fascination as the knife opened up the dessert to reveal a dark red fruity inside, like a terrible wound. Josie felt her gorge rise and for one moment thought she was going to be sick.

'An old air force friend of Chris's. They were in France together. They flew together. And he was a friend of Peter's too. He rang up to say how sorry he was about Chris. He'd just heard. But he didn't know about Peter. The strange thing was that he said he saw Chris on Friday night in London and he asked Chris after Peter and Chris said Peter was fine. But Chris knew Peter was dead.'

'In London? What was Chris doing in London?'

'He said he had to see someone that night. And he gave Josie a lift home to Wimbledon, didn't he, Josie?'

Josie felt her eyes boring into her, as if the woman could see through her head and out the other side. She felt like a hare hypnotized by a weasel. Incapable of thought or word. She felt her jaw drop open.

'Did he seem disturbed that night, Josie? About Peter? Did he talk about Peter?'

'N–no.'

'Not at all?'

'Only to say he was . . . dead.'

'And he drove you straight to Wimbledon and put you down outside your house?'

'Yes,' Josie whispered.

She could feel the flames burning her cheeks as she lied. She was on her way to hell. How did the woman know Chris had taken her to London? The village grapevine was infallible.

'Who did he have to see? Do you know?'

'No, I don't know.' Groping at straws she added, 'He wore his best uniform. For seeing someone, he said.'

'So what did he do? Put you down at your house and drive off to see this someone?'

'I – yes. He put me down.'

'Eunice, is this all right for you? Not too much?' She handed her sister a plate of meringue.

'Yes, dear, how lovely, what a treat!'

'Tilly is a real wizard when it comes to meringue. I can never get it to rise up.'

Josie could feel her heart thudding up in her throat. The woman was playing with her like a cat with a mouse, she thought. She had always wondered how the mouse felt. Now she knew. As expected, the big purring cat came back to her with an icy smile.

'You must have been the last person to be with him, apart from this person we know nothing about. Was he in a good mood?'

'Yes, he was happy,' Josie stuttered.

'How could he have been happy, when Peter had just been killed?' Coming in for the kill, the voice was harsh.

'He said he didn't want to talk about Peter. He couldn't—'

She was being interrogated like a German prisoner. Everyone round the table seemed to be hanging on her words, mouths open, and Mrs Patterson had assumed a terrifying mien. She seemed to have grown. No longer a cat, she was a vulture. Her eyes glittered. Josie felt her head whirling and her brain told her she had drunk too much. This wasn't happening!

'You see, this man on the phone said he'd met Chris in a dance hall in Mayfair. And he said he had a girl with him. But if he had already dropped you off at

236

home, I suppose . . . did he say anything about meeting a girl?' Josie gulped.

'No.'

She thought she was going to pass out. It was like a nightmare, all the faces round the table turned on her, their eyes popping.

She knew what was coming. Now Mrs Patterson was a huge cat again, and she had the little mouse trembling in her paws.

'I think the girl was you.'

'Ma, this isn't fair.'

The voice was Jumbo's.

'It's private, what Chris did that night. If he'd wanted you to know, he'd have told you. He just wanted to get away, because of Peter. You can see how he felt.'

'One is curious about his last hours, that's all. It puts one in the picture.'

Mrs Patterson ignored Jumbo.

'If it's true, we don't hold it against you, you understand,' she said directly to Josie. 'We would just like to know.'

Oh, but she did hold it against her, Josie could see! She could see the icy glitter in her eyes, that Chris preferred her to his austere home, that he liked seeing her in the pub rather than come home, that he held her in his arms, that he loved her! Oh, he had loved her!

She burst out crying, she could not help herself. Not just quiet, reverent sobs but a wild loud wail that made them all drop their spoons with a clatter.

'He loved me! He loved me! That's why he took me, so that we could be together! He loved me!' she screamed.

Her voice was so shrill it cracked, and her proclamation ended in a series of choking coughs. She pushed back her chair, so violently that it fell over, and rushed for the door. Out in the hall, sobbing and choking, she wrestled with the bolts on the front door, unable to get it open.

'Josie!'

Jumbo was there, grabbing her by the shoulders, pulling her away.

'Stop it! Stop it!'

'Let me out! Let me out!' she shrieked.

He clicked back the bolt. But before she could flee he got hold of her arm and stopped her. He hopped outside and slammed it shut behind them. Holding her by both shoulders he shook her hard.

'For God's sake, Josie, calm down! Don't cry, don't cry!'

All the stuffing seemed to go out of her so that she would have fallen if he had not held her. He wrapped his arms round her and held her head against his chest with his big calloused hand, stroking her hair.

'My little Josie, it's all right! It's all right. Yes, he did love you, I know he did. You will have him for always, all yours, in your heart. Lucky, lucky Chris.'

Long afterards, when she was sane, Jumbo's words came back to her, the generosity overwhelming her.

After how she had treated him! But now the great warmth of his dear person was a cloak of comfort round her, sobbing on the doorstep. Her hysteria died down, and she buried her face in his chest.

'I loved him so! I loved him!' she kept hiccuping inanely, senseless of the hurt to Jumbo.

He held her tenderly, kissing her hair and her wet face. 'I know, I know, Josie. Don't cry else we'll all be at it.'

His warm enfolding arms were what she so desperately needed: comfort and understanding at last with someone who shared her grief. Yet she knew that she was hurting him now as badly as anyone could, because she knew he loved her as much as she loved Chris.

In the frosty night air they stood coming to terms with the empty sky, its cruelties, their stupid situation, the total unfairness of life, all the things that could not be put into words, and their whole, hopeless confusion held them comforting each other while the dinner party continued without them.

There was complete silence round the dinner table. Mrs Patterson went on cutting up the meringue.

'Robert?'

She passed the plate.

'Thank you.'

She put the last slice down in front of her husband and laid her hand on his for the signal, as always. He picked up his spoon.

'That was unwise of you, my dear,' he said. 'So much hurt. They are so young. They can't cope.'

'They have to learn! Her hurt is not a fraction of mine. How can it be? She has no idea, thinking she loves him. How long since they met? All of a few weeks. Why did Jumbo ask her here tonight? She has no place here.'

Her voice was shaking. Her sister and husband applied themselves diligently to their meringue.

Her husband put out a hesitant hand and found her shoulder. He patted her as if she were one of his labradors.

'Chris was looking for comfort, after Peter. It didn't mean anything. A girl, drink, a dance – that's how they cope with it. The girl doesn't mean anything.'

'She thinks she does!'

'Darling, don't upset yourself. It can't have been serious. Just getting over Peter. He didn't know he was going to die.'

'I think he did.'

There was a long silence. They all concentrated on eating. Robert picked up his wine glass and took a long swig, coughed into the silence. Their spoons clinked on the priceless Royal Derby dishes.

'I think there are some things not worth discussing,' the colonel said.

He put down his spoon.

'I want a brandy. And you, Robert?'

'Yes . . . I think a double.'

Chapter Twenty

Flight Officer Josephine Marsden pushed her way through the crowded streets, marvelling as ever at the mix of taxis, donkey carts, army staff cars, gharris pulled by skinny horses, and overbearing, klaxon-blaring trams that made up the Cairo traffic. The heat was blistering. Under her formal uniform sweat trickled down between her shoulder-blades. Oh, for a cool drink and the shade of a palm tree in a quiet courtyard! But she had to hurry: she was late for her rendezvous.

Men and women of all nationalities thronged the streets – hundreds of men in uniform, men in business suits, in flowing white jellabas, in kaftans, in oil-stained dungarees, and women covered all in black, just their dark eyes looking out, or women in pre-war Parisian fashion, here and there a colourful eastern sari, and everywhere red fezes bobbing like bright berries and people chattering in all the languages of the world. What a melting-pot, Cairo at the end of the war! Josie had learned her way around and loved it and dreaded the ending of her peripatetic life now that it was so near. Not that a more temperate climate than Cairo would come amiss. It was hard to recall that summer showers must now be enlivening Wimbledon, scenting the air with the smell of damp earth and freshly unfurled leaves. Sometimes home-sickness stabbed, jolted by a random fragment of conversation or a homely smell, a memory thrown up by a photo or mention of a name. But mostly her job consumed her as it did them all. Overworked and often over-tired, she nevertheless loved the life unreservedly.

Her friend Barbara was waiting for her in the foyer of the busy Shepheard's Hotel. Like Josie she was in WAAF officers' uniform. They found a table in a quiet corner under a fan and ordered cool drinks from a handsome young Egyptian waiter.

'I shall be twenty-one next month,' Josie said, 'And I don't know whether I shall have a party here or at home. The war can't possibly last much longer.'

'God knows what happens next. Nobody knows.'

'I don't want to go anywhere. I've forgotten how to think for myself.'

'Strange, isn't it? I suppose we go back to what we were doing before. It doesn't seem possible – to work in an office near Victoria station.'

'Art school. How can I start again? It's not possible.'

'You needn't have joined up if you were at college. Not till you'd finished, anyway.'

'No, but I wanted to. It seemed stupid to miss it. I

had no one to keep me at home. And I wasn't much good anyway.'

'It's something you can always do, like music. You don't have to have a degree in it, after all.'

'No. I'll just be a lady water colourist in my spare time. That will suit me nicely. But spare time from what?'

'I imagine it'll be hard to get a job, thousands of us all coming back. And the men too. How on earth can they go back to their offices after storming Monte Cassino, dropping bombs on Germany, getting torpedoed and all that? They'll go mad. I suppose I'll marry Bob when he comes out, and that'll be two of us out of work. I can't see him settling down in suburbia.'

'Maybe it will be better out here, South Africa perhaps, or Kenya or somewhere.'

'Lots of people think that. It's very dreary in England just now, so everyone says when they come back from leave. Depends what you've got to go home for, I suppose, or who, more like.'

'Nobody, save my parents.'

'You shouldn't be alone! You could have anyone you want, especially lovely Tony. What's wrong with you?'

'Just playing around, going out with them, having fun – that's all right. I've never stayed in moping, have I?'

'No. But what's wrong with Tony? He's mad about you, everyone knows.'

Josie shrugged. 'Yes, he's sweet. But he doesn't measure up.'

243

'Up to whom?'

'Oh, just dreams. No one in particular.'

'I bet you'll never meet so many blokes when you're back home. If you miss your chance now – think of it – with twenty-one looming.'

'An old maid!'

They both laughed. Barbara's Bob was an amiable transport officer. With his pal Tony making a foursome they had had many good nights out dancing and drinking and lying on the beach at Alexandria when they had a bit of leave. Josie could see good-natured Barbara and laid-back Bob bringing up a nice family back at home, discussing schools, saving for holidays – in spite of Barbara's pessimism. But she couldn't see it for herself. Not with Tony, not with anyone.

Lying on a beach with Chris, walking with him hand in hand in some paradise where there was no war, no fighting, no Hurricane waiting on the tarmac . . . But she told herself a love affair of five years ago which lasted all of a bare few weeks was just a farce. She could not speak of this to Barbara: it was too ludicrous. But why had it stayed with her when her life since had been packed with incident, with excitement, with caring, glamorous people, heady foreign places and incessant travel? When she met Chris she had been a witless child. Had that been the attraction for him, her innocence? She sometimes thought that to him at that time she represented the unattainable, that his first stupefied vision of her in his state of half consciousness, framed by a landscape of paradise, had completely coloured his later infatuation. For what else could it have been other than infatuation? The memory of it should have faded by now but it hadn't. It was what held her back from committing herself to anyone else. Really stupid. As Barbara said, she was nearly an old maid. Nearly everyone was married by the time they were twenty-one.

'There's a dance here tonight,' Barbara said. 'Are you coming?'

'That's what I want to see you about. I said I would but now I think I've got to drive the old codger to Port Said tonight. He threw it at me without warning, as usual. Can you warn Tony?'

'OK. But if you can make it, try. Maybe something else will turn up for him. They're running round in circles half the time.'

'Yes. I know.' Josie looked at her watch and stood up. 'I must go. I'm on duty at twelve.'

She left Barbara sitting waiting for her boyfriend and went out through the foyer. On her way out she glanced at the correspondence waiting to be collected – nothing for her, but a buff envelope caught her eye, addressed to Patterson. The name jumped out at her. Pattersons were two a penny but it made her catch her breath for a moment. She looked more closely.

'*Wing Commander C. Patterson*', she read. The address was care of Shepheard's Hotel.

In spite of knowing it was impossible, she felt suddenly dizzy at the sight of the name. She *knew* it was impossible. Auntie Betty still wrote to her at intervals, and it surely would have been the news of the century if he had turned up. She would have been told. She knew that after three months or so hope had faded and Auntie Betty had reported that there had been a memorial service in the church which had caused quite a little excitement, such smart people attending, and after that no more.

All the same, she could not stop herself from enquiring at the desk after Wing Commander C. Patterson. The receptionist gave her a room number but said he was out.

'Is he staying long?'

'There's no date for departure.'

Josie had to hurry back to camp but resolved to enquire after the Wing Commander later. He might have been there for months, for all she knew. But after the first shock she calmed down and knew that her excitement was for nothing. She tried to put it to the back of her mind but it kept jumping out at her. She resolved to go back as soon as she could and dampen her ardour by finding that the Wing Commander was a stuffy old trout whose Christian name was Cuthbert, but her boss decreed otherwise and she had to stay in Port Said for several days, and then drive on to Alexandria. Here by chance she met Barbara again with Bob and Tony, up for a free weekend. They went for drinks at a bar overlooking the harbour, and toasted the reported death of Hitler. All was frantic activity and the talk was all of demobilization.

'We could be home in a month,' Barbara declared.

'Women will be the first to go. Back to the kitchen sink where we belong!'

For the first time Josie felt a qualm of fear for her future. The thought of going back to her parents was anathema. Impossible! And what sort of a job was she fit for? None in civvy street at all. No one would employ a female driver, even one who could drive anything from a jeep to a fifteen-ton truck.

Barbara and Bob were engaged, with a ring to prove it. That night Tony proposed (again) to Josie, and for the first time Josie wavered. They sat together on a balcony overlooking the sea and watched a half-moon etching a glittering path towards them over the silky Mediterranean. A few boats out of the harbour threw up diamonds of phosphorescence in their wake, their engines thrumming softly in the windless night. Softly from a ballroom echoed the seductive Glenn Miller tune 'In the Mood' that they all danced to, and from a white jasmine climbing up over the terrace a heady scent set a scene so romantic that it had to be remarked on.

'You'd propose to anyone tonight, after a couple of gins,' Josie said wryly.

'And anyone would accept, after a couple of gins.'

He was a sweetie, she had to admit, kind and easy-going. He reckoned he had a job to go back to in school-mastering and was looking forward to it. He was twenty-five and had spent an uneventful war filtering intelligence – killing by paperwork, as he described it. He would make a good husband. But she didn't love him. Did it matter?

Josie sighed. 'I'm really stupid, I'm sorry. It's just that . . .' Her voice faded. Impossible.

'There's someone else?'

'Such a long time ago. It's so stupid. He was killed. I was only a kid.'

She would never forget him, not ever. But she couldn't allow the memory to blight her whole life; it didn't make sense.

'Look, I won't say no. But can we wait a little longer, till we see what's happening? I haven't thought about it seriously. I need time.'

'You don't love me, I know that. But you like me, and I love you. It's not a hopeless basis for a marriage, after all. We get on, we're good friends.'

'Yes, I know.'

Seeing his earnest face in the moonlight, the blond head of hair silvered, the eyes so pleading, she was hard put not to give in. It would work, he was perfect husband material: kind, intelligent, honest and loyal. One could not ask for more. But of course she did, remembering.

'I'll decide when we get back. Promise. In a few days.'

Afterwards she wondered if seeing the name on that letter, Wing Commader C. Patterson, was really what had stopped her from agreeing. If she were to sort that and meet Cuthbert, as she now thought of him, it might lay the ghost of times past. The thought pleased her, gave her hope. The more she thought of going back to England with Tony and making a future together, the more it seemed the sensible thing to do.

Driving back to Cairo with her boss, an elderly air marshall who organized supplies, she was impatient to call back at the hotel. The journey was as ghastly as ever, the throttling heat, the clouds of dust, the awful road lined with broken-down trucks and all the litter of war combining to make the hundred or so miles feel like five hundred. The air marshall passed a water bottle at regular intervals and snored stertorously in between. He had been in the services all his life and knew how to make the best of any situation, an easy and kindly man to work for. He had flown a Sopwith Camel in the last war just like Biggles, although it was hard to see him in the role of hero now, his hair having thinned and his nose reddened with drink. Josie knew she had been lucky in the postings that had come her way. Terrible though the war was, it had provided unbelievable opportunities to the suburban stick-in-the-muds like herself. Even Maureen had joined up and worked on a gun battery, forgetting poor Tom, who had been killed at El Alamein. She wrote at intervals about her good times with American soldiers and was currently going out with an ex-cowboy from Wyoming.

She got back to base in the afternoon and decided to go straight to Shepheard's Hotel to beard Cuthbert. He might be in before going out to dinner – it was the most likely time. She bathed and changed and made herself look as respectable as possible and, in spite of knowing in her heart that Wing Commander C. Patterson couldn't possibly be Chris, she found that she was feeling sick with nervous tension. Her hands were trembling as she applied her lipstick. Make-up was tricky when one sweated so freely but with luck it would last out until she got to the hotel. If he wasn't in she would wait for him. She couldn't go on in this state of indecision. Another day and – who knows? – he might be posted away, never to be traced again. The thought of that, now that she was so keyed up, was unbearable. *C. Patterson – who are you?*

Plunging back into the mêlée of the city, her agitation grew. By the time she got to the hotel she was in a fever of impatience. If he was out she would wait but how she would be able to contain herself she did not know. He might be on a week's trip to Ismailia or Kabrit or anywhere, just as she had been away for several days. People came and went in Cairo, a never-ending stew of faces, half-remembered, half-forgotten.

She went up to the reception desk.

'Wing Commander Patterson? Is he in?'

The young Egyptian consulted the keyboard behind him and nodded.

'Yes, madam. Room two hundred and three. Third floor.'

Josie nearly swooned away on the spot. Having convinced herself of the hopelessness of her quest she was now almost too terrified to move. But of course he was any old Patterson! There were thousands of

250

them. Swearing to herself that this was the truth she bent her steps towards the staircase. No lift for her, she needed time. Slowly, slowly, the sweat beading her face, she approached room two hundred and three.

She stood outside for a full minute, listening. Silence within. Perhaps he was asleep? She would wake him and confront an angry, red-faced officer. He would bawl her out.

She raised her arm, swallowed. She tapped, so gently that he could not possibly hear. She waited again.

Oh, come on! she said to herself and knocked loudly. He could not help but hear.

The door opened. A tall figure stood against the light, his features hard to make out. But she knew him. She thought she would pass out.

'Josie!'

'Jumbo! Oh, Jumbo!'

'Josie!'

He held out out his arms and held her up, drew her into the room and kicked the door shut behind him. Josie was crying and laughing at the same time, incredulous.

'I thought – I didn't expect . . .'

'How did you know I was here?'

'I didn't. I just saw your name on the letter board. I just thought – I thought it was worth a try, to see if – if . . .'

'If I was Chris?'

'Yes.'

'Are you disappointed?'

'No, oh no! I can't believe it! That it should be you! I expected a cross old man, you know – anybody!'

'I didn't know you were out here. I knew you had joined the WAAFs, but nothing else. I had no idea.'

Josie, recovering from the shock, was now filled with an overwhelming relief and joy to be with Jumbo again. It was a possibility she had never considered.

'The C – what does it stand for?'

'Clarence. I told you it was too awful to tell you. Chris did me a good turn calling me Jumbo.'

'Oh, I can't believe it! How wonderful to see you again!'

Josie had to sit down, her legs suddenly all trembly. Jumbo was all concern, fetching her a drink (Whatever was it? Its reviving qualities were remarkable) and seating her in a long chair in the window. His suite was elegant, the high windows looking out over the Nile, and thankfully in shade at last as the sun made its welcome descent into the desert. A great wash of happiness spread over Josie, possibly initiated by the drink, but now strengthened by the mere sight of Jumbo's familiar face. He was no longer the gangly youth she remembered but a spruce and elegant officer in a well-cut uniform with – she noticed quickly – pilot's wings on his breast and, like Chris, the purple and white striped medal ribbon of the DFC. He moved easily, hardly revealing his injury, a far cry from the last time she had seen him. It seemed so long ago. So much had happened.

'You did what you wanted,' she said. 'I knew you would.'

'Yes, it worked out. They were good to me. I had to measure up. But I didn't think I could emulate Chris so I went into bombers, not fighters, and was lucky to come through. After my last tour I was sent here for a rest and now it looks as if the rest will be permanent.'

'Yes, seems like it's going home time. Nobody seems to know what happens next.'

'No. I suspect they'll be getting rid of us as fast as possible. Tell me what you've been doing.'

Josie told him about her life in the WAAFs and Jumbo told her about his uphill task to get accepted into the life he wanted.

'I just had to prove I could do it, then they couldn't turn me down. But it was tough. Tough enough just to get your wings as a pilot without people putting you down, telling you to get a desk job, belittling you. I had my father behind me, luckily, as an example. He didn't pull strings – I did it on my own. And Chris too, having Chris – it was for him, because he always believed in me.'

'Nobody ever heard any more, what happened to Chris?'

'No.'

Jumbo looked thoughtfully at his empty glass and said, 'I think you hoped the C stood for Chris.'

Josie could not answer. She felt her cheeks flushing, bit her lip. She couldn't lie. She parried the question.

'It never occurred to me that it could be you. I

thought it was worth a try, but expected a complete stranger.'

'I knew you'd fallen in love with him. Perhaps before you knew it yourself.'

Josie could not defend herself. 'I was loving you, before he came.'

'Yes, you were nearly loving me. It was going to work. But we were only kids, after all, we met too soon. Chris knew that I really cared about you, not like the other silly girls he had pinched from me in the past. I told him. I sometimes think, you know, that perhaps . . .' His voice faded.

Josie had sometimes thought it too. She waited.

'It was so strange. He knew he was low on fuel, but he didn't turn back.'

'In the excitement of a dogfight they didn't, sometimes.'

'The new kids, perhaps. Not Chris. He had survived so long by knowing when to give best. He had a terrible conscience about my leg, and then, you see, I told him how much I loved you and he realized what he had done to me in that department, stolen you away, and it makes me wonder sometimes . . . the fact that he was at the end of his tether anyway, and Peter going – that was a terrible blow. Perhaps he had had enough.'

'We shall never know. But it has crossed my mind too.'

'We've never spoken of it at home, but I think my mother thought that. I know he felt terrible about coming between you and me. The last time I saw him – I said things to him that I've regretted ever since. The last words I spoke to him: I said I hoped he would never come back. I've had to live with that.'

Josie was shocked, horrified by the damage she had done. What a stupid, ignorant girl she had been! What a terrible ending to the closest friendship between brothers she had ever seen! But her hopeless heart, even seeing Jumbo's distress, jumped to wondering if Chris had told him that he loved her in return, or had he just said sorry for the silly girl falling for him when he had appeared on the scene, the handsome hero? Had he told Jumbo how much he had loved her? Had he loved her? Josie sometimes thought the affair which had so affected her life was a figment of her imagination. The dreamlike first meeting, his enfolding arms on the dance-floor of the smoochy, smoky little club in Mayfair which she had relived so many times, the cold, dear grass on Wimbledon Common before the anguished parting . . . Now that she had seen so much of life and fleeting love-affairs in the forces she saw that it was nothing special, it was happening all the time. Save that it had been the most special thing that had ever happened to her and she couldn't bear for it to have been just a run-of-the-mill bit of fun for Chris. In her most secret heart she had always thought he might have died for loving her. Now Jumbo was suggesting Chris might have died because of her loving him instead of Jumbo.

Now he was dead they would never know the truth of it.

But she couldn't help herself.

'Did he say that he loved me?'

Jumbo looked surprised.

'No, he didn't.' And then, after a pause, 'Did he?'

Josie shook her head. She could not answer.

'He never loved a girl that I know of. Only for a quick fling, you know. He wasn't particularly interested in girls – too much to do. Climbing, flying, the motorbike. All those blokes' things.'

He passed her a cigarette and she took it, bending her head to the proffered lighter. It was best to forget. Tony was a good bet, after all, safe and kind.

'And you?' she asked.

'No, only you. I've only ever loved you.'

Shocked, she looked up into his face. It was for a moment the face of the young, hopping Jumbo, freckled and smiling, the grey-green eyes full of confidence and fun. Then, almost at once, she saw the truth: a face scarred by loss, the face of a bomber pilot on recuperative leave, lined long before its time, tired and haggard. But in the eyes there was the funny light she remembered.

'Don't look so surprised.'

She laughed.

'You might not love me now. I've changed. You've changed. Everything is different.'

'I grant you. But we can meet as strangers and see if we like each other. There are no rules in this life. Can

I take you out to dinner tonight, Flight Officer Marsden? An assessment job? Are you free?'

'Yes. Yes, I'm free.'

'We might both be disappointed. Expect nothing. Time has been cruel.'

'I know that.'

'And I'm packing up to leave. My time is up here but there are no more bombs to drop, so I've no idea what we'll be up to. It might just be ships passing in the night, Josie, you know how things are. And you too, I expect you'll be away shortly. But it will be fun to catch up with things, and we can keep in touch whatever happens.'

'Cuthbert!' Josie laughed. 'I told myself the C stood for Cuthbert and you'd be a red-nosed old buffer I'd be waking up. I never dreamed—'

'It was your old Jumbo!'

'Clarence!'

'They call me Clarry. Clarry the lamb. I haven't a very fierce reputation, I'm afraid. But there, they always find me a nice table here. I'll get myself spruced up and we'll go down. Just wait there a tick and I'll be with you.'

Josie smoked her cigarette looking out on Cairo, feeling suddenly that her whole life was spread there higgledy-piggledy like the great seething city, chance and coincidence driving it, the future inscrutable, the past a mess. Anything could happen.

Wait and see.

Chapter Twenty-One

Two weeks later Jumbo was posted home. The war was over. He was not sorry to be leaving the heat and stench of the Middle East, even if it meant leaving Josie behind for a short time. The night before, at their parting dinner, he had given her a beautiful ruby and diamond engagement ring.

Turning it on her finger, flushed with happiness, she said, 'This is the first valuable thing I've ever had. When I went to stay with Auntie Betty, when I first met you, all my possessions went in one little suitcase. And it's no different now. Even when our house was bombed, the only thing I regretted losing was a blue china rabbit. I've never had anything.'

'It's good to travel light. You've nothing to lose.'

'I shall never lose this. It's much too good for me.'

'Nothing's too good for you.'

Their relationship had established itself as if no time had passed. Considering all that had happened, Jumbo thought it strange and infinitely satisfying. He had taken plenty of girls out but never loved any of them, measuring them up to his brief summer with Josie. Before Chris. It did not do to be serious about a girl when the job was so dangerous. But all that was over now, thank God. There was everything to look forward to. Josie was coming back to England a week after himself and would meet him at home. What his mother would say to having Josie as a daughter-in-law he had rather not wanted to think about. His mother would consider her insufficiently well-bred, her ideas on human beings grounded in her knowledge of breeding horses. But the war had put paid to such entrenched social standings: his mother would not be aware of that. She would have to learn. Poor old Ma. If nothing else, Jumbo's war had given him an authority he had never aspired to before. There had been situations far more frightening than facing his mother. It made him laugh to think what a naive idiot he had been in those days.

A boy came to collect his bags and tell him his taxi was waiting. He had a last look round, picked up his key and went down to the reception. The man behind the desk said, 'There's post for you, sir.'

He handed over three envelopes. Two buff letters of no account, and one much travelled airmail letter. He looked at this curiously and as he recognized the writing he almost keeled over with shock. A frisson of emotion shook him, so weird a mixture of joy and horror that he exclaimed out loud.

'Oh my God!'

He tried to pretend that he was mistaken, but he knew he wasn't.

'Your taxi is waiting, sir,' said the boy, wanting a tip.

Jumbo fumbled absently in his pocket. He followed the boy out and scrambled into the waiting car, clutching the flimsy letter in his shaking, sweating hands. He lay back in the seat, not daring to open it. But scrutiny of the envelope showed that it came from India, which calmed him a fraction.

'Chris, oh Chris, what are you doing to me?' he breathed. 'How can you come back now?'

Five years! Thank God he was alone with no one to witness his funk. A month ago and he would have been ecstatic with joy – why, oh why, now?

He got out a penknife and carefully slit the letter open. The all -too-familiar scrawl, compressed with difficulty, leaped off the page.

Jumbo, old chap,

I have been in two minds for so long as to whether I should write this letter, but I know I must, come what may. Whether you tell our parents I am still alive or not is up to you, but you must see that technically I am a deserter and I think that might be too much for our father. If I come back I shall be court-martialled and sent to prison, and I could not bear that. And nor, I think, could our parents.

I did mean to finish myself off, but at the last moment I was too chicken. I was about to go in when I saw a small ship and on a coward's impulse I jumped out and parachuted down quite close. Of course they took me on board. It was a Spanish ship bound for the Argentine, not very friendly – neutral officially but definitely with German sympathies. They didn't bother to report my presence to anyone and dumped me off without ceremony in Rio. That was where I decided to go AWOL. Wrong, I know. I've no excuse. Only that I've always wanted to climb in the Andes. And, seeing those mountains – well, Jumbo, I don't have to explain to you. I forgot everything and went bush. I am not proud of myself.

There isn't room here to tell you all my adventures but over the years I've flown for a living, any old transports any old where, got false papers, a false name, avoided service areas like the plague and now landed up in the Himalayas, where we always planned to go. I just thought there might be a way of your joining me here for a spot of climbing now the war is over. You needn't say who you're going to meet, just make something up. I can't say how much I miss you, Jumbo. When Peter went, and after my tangle with your sweet little girl, it made me want to finish everything, I was so ashamed of what I had done. I can't make any excuses for my behaviour.

I came across someone recently who talked about you and I found out how you'd made it. I always knew you would: I found your whereabouts after a bit of subterfuge (I am very good at subterfuge these days) and so am writing. Maybe you have moved on and this letter will never find you.

261

Perhaps for the best, I don't know. But it's worth a try. I don't really expect anything.

Your loving brother, Chris.

Tears trickled down Jumbo's cheeks. He was shaking all over now, and then sobbing openly, his old love for Chris overwhelming him. But the timing of the letter was terrible. The taxi driver thought the letter announced a death, not a life, but wasn't unused to seeing such emotions displayed in these emotional times and kept his eyes on the road. Jumbo looked out at the teeming traffic blocking their way, aware that the aeroplane he was to catch would bear him half a world farther away from Chris. In Cairo, the Himalayas were not so far away. There was an address scribbled on the letter, care of someone with an Indian name.

'Chris, oh Chris, what have you done?' he groaned.

He knew that to let Josie know of this letter would be to lose her. If not to lose her, to put her in an impossible quandary. Their marriage would never be safe if she knew Chris was still alive. Or so he thought. He couldn't be sure. She was loyal and honest and would not let him down, but her heart was under no such discipline and would do what it willed. No one could change that.

He wondered whether to change his plans and make a trip to India before Josie came home. But his parents were expecting him, would be there to meet him off the plane, and how on earth would he be able to explain his sudden change of plan and then, once home, cover up his experience? Chris had put a burden on him heavier than he thought he could bear. It was impossible to know whether telling his parents of Chris's survival would be a blessing or a cross of shame too much for them. They were so imbued with Victorian attitudes of duty and honour. But that was a decision he must take, and to tell them would mean Josie knowing too. It was impossible. His own happiness depended on Josie not knowing.

The thoughts chased themselves through his stunned brain. If only he had walked out without receiving the letter! He had been so happy, full of optimism, longing to be back in England again, his mind full of the pleasures of wandering through his old haunts, lying by the lake, walking the dogs, waiting for Josie. He had plans for trying to get his hands on the old manor: it was hardly worth anything now and to own even the ruin would enchant him. And Josie too, he knew. The gratuity due to him would probably cover it. He had dreamed all this up in the last week or two. Meeting Josie again had revived all his old rose-tinted plans for the future, brought them into focus as real possibilities rather than dreams.

The first shock overcome, he lay back in the bone-shaking seat of the taxi and more calmly considered his options. Going to India now, this minute, was not one of them, he realized with reluctance, although it was what he most wanted to do. To see Chris again, older no doubt in every way – to have survived as he had – but still with his enthusiasms, courage and sheer fun presence was a longing he found hard to shrug off. But perhaps, he thought, later . . . much later when relationships at home were consolidated (hopefully) and life was calm again, he could reconsider a meeting with Chris, or alternatively take the decision that it was impossible. Procrastinate. Write back? He groaned out loud. How could he not? Chris, oh Chris, what have you done to me? There was no one to confide in. It was his pigeon entirely, and a crushing burden.

The airfield was a maelstrom of activity with troops returning home. In the fierce heat the aircraft on the tarmac glittered like great dragonflies, their engines driving storms of dust into the blazing air. The cool of England was a dream – almost impossible to believe that it was coming true. And Josie, dear Josie, soon on her way to join him. Jumbo let himself be elbowed into the queue, his mind disengaged. All his dearest ambitions within his grasp: a few more steps into the plane and he was on his way.

He took the letter and tore it into tiny pieces and, as he climbed the steps into the aeroplane, threw them down onto the tarmac. They whooshed away in a cloud of dust and with them, he felt, went half of him.

But the half that was left would grow whole in time. That was the way of things.